Hallie felt really, truly awful.

She didn't want to be doing this, didn't want to take on this giant of a man who had the fiercest eyebrows she'd ever seen, and who had every right to be using the phone.

But the note said to be at this very pay phone, outside Promise Hardware, at ten sharp. So, rights and fierce eyebrows aside, she had no choice but to make him hang up.

The man was still glaring at her. Oh, dear, what to do? What to do? Lowering her gaze, she was greeted by the sight of a well-used leather briefcase on the sidewalk between his feet—*his* briefcase.

Without thinking, she reached down, grabbed it and—much to his surprise—hurried away. She saw the moment he left the phone dangling to come charging after her. Quickly she tossed the briefcase into the alleyway, watched him go after it, then she dashed back to the phone.

Dear Reader,

If you're like me, you can't get enough heartwarming love stories and real-life fairy tales that end happily ever after. You'll find what you need and so much more with Silhouette Romance each month.

This month you're in for an extra treat. Bestselling author Susan Meier kicks off MARRYING THE BOSS'S DAUGHTER—the brand-new six-book series written exclusively for Silhouette Romance. In this launch title, *Love, Your Secret Admirer* (#1684), our favorite matchmaking heiress helps a naive secretary snare her boss's attention with an eye-catching makeover.

A sexy rancher discovers love and the son he never knew, when he matches wits with a beautiful teacher, in *What a Woman Should Know* (#1685) by Cara Colter. And a not-so plain Jane captures a royal heart, in *To Kiss a Sheik* (#1686) by Teresa Southwick, the second of three titles in her sultry DESERT BRIDES miniseries.

Debrah Morris brings you a love story of two lifetimes, in *When Lightning Strikes Twice* (#1687), the newest paranormal love story in the SOULMATES series. And sparks sizzle between an innocent curator—with a big secret—and the town's new lawman, in *Ransom* (#1688) by Diane Pershing. Will a seamstress's new beau still love her when he learns she is an undercover heiress? Find out in *The Bridal Chronicles* (#1689) by Lissa Manley.

Be my guest and feed your need for tender and lighthearted romance with all six of this month's great new love stories from Silhouette Romance.

Enjoy!

Mavis C. Allen
Associate Senior Editor, Silhouette Romance

Please address questions and book requests to:
Silhouette Reader Service
U.S.: 3010 Walden Ave., P.O. Box 1325, Buffalo, NY 14269
Canadian: P.O. Box 609, Fort Erie, Ont. L2A 5X3

Ransom

DIANE PERSHING

SILHOUETTE *Romance*®

Published by Silhouette Books

America's Publisher of Contemporary Romance

Thanks go to the enchanting Pacific Grove, California,
and its Heritage Society. I borrowed liberally from
the town's history when creating my fictional
town of Promise. However, all of the book's characters
and dialog, its buildings and streets,
are products of my humble imagination.

 SILHOUETTE BOOKS

ISBN 0-373-19688-1

RANSOM

This edition published by arrangement with Harlequin Books S.A.

® and TM are trademarks of Harlequin Books S.A., used under license.
Trademarks indicated with ® are registered in the United States Patent
and Trademark Office, the Canadian Trade Marks Office and in other
countries.

Visit Silhouette at www.eHarlequin.com

Printed in U.S.A.

DIANE PERSHING

cannot remember a time when she didn't have her nose buried in a book. As a child, she would cheat the bedtime curfew by snuggling under the covers with her teddy bear, a flashlight and a forbidden (i.e., a grown-up) novel. Her mother warned her that she would ruin her eyes, but so far, they still work. Diane has had many careers—singer, actress, film critic, disc jockey, TV writer, to name a few. Currently she divides her time between writing romances and doing voice-overs. (You can hear her as Poison Ivy on the *Batman* cartoon.) She lives in Los Angeles, and promises she is only slightly affected. Her two children, Morgan Rose and Ben, have just completed college, and Diane looks forward to writing and acting until she expires, or people stop hiring her, whichever comes first. She loves to hear from readers, so please write to her at P.O. Box 67424, Los Angeles, CA 90067.

SALLIE

Bring $25,000 in small bills to the Phone

booth outside Promise hardware.

ten sharp.

If you get involved with the law,

the doll gets it!

Chapter One

"Please hold."

"But I—"

Marc ended his protest with a muttered curse as the sounds of some bass-heavy street rap selection came blasting through the phone's receiver. He had to hold the damn thing away from his ear before it caused permanent hearing loss. Even so, his toe kept time on the sidewalk; he had a lot of frustrated energy today, and it had to go somewhere.

Shoulder propped against the plastic side of the phone booth, he forced himself to gaze around, to take in the town's main street and its row of well-maintained storefronts, the line of graceful trees along the curbside, the small town square, replete with benches, blooming flower beds, and, at its center, a stone fountain housing a plump, naked cherub that gushed water from its mouth.

No doubt about it, Promise was a pretty little town,

and he'd made a good decision to begin his life as a civilian here…or had he?

Right now, he wasn't sure. He'd been on this pay phone, on hold ninety percent of the time, for well over half an hour now. If he hadn't needed to get his phones installed ASAP, he would long ago have demanded to speak to someone in management and—assuming a real live human being actually worked there—would have ripped them a new ear hole.

The music changed now to some nasal young female complaining about a boy who wouldn't notice her. No wonder. If Marc had to wake up to that whine every morning, he'd have dumped her before the first date started.

He cursed again, ground his teeth one more time, then caught himself. Uh-oh. Better watch it, he told himself. The signs were there. He forced himself to take in a couple of deep breaths, forced himself to exhale each of them slowly, to a count of ten. He had a temper, knew it and kept it under wraps as much as possible. But it had been a bad day, a very bad day, and he wasn't in the mood to be patient, a character quality he didn't possess much of anyway. What he needed was a distraction.

And just like that, he got one.

A woman, about a block and a half away and walking briskly toward him. It was the hair that drew his attention first. Strawberry-blond and curly, in the bright morning sunlight it surrounded her face like a cloud of cotton candy. Her pace was determined and purposeful, and it made her hair bounce as she walked, which made him smile. For the first time that day.

As she crossed the street and drew closer, Marc took in the fact that she wore black slacks, a plain white blouse and tennis shoes, that she was slim and about five four. He wondered where she was headed with such fierce purpose. Another few strides brought her closer and he got the impression of an ordinary-looking face which seemed flushed from exercise. She was breathing heavily, as though she'd run most of the way here, and had only dialed it back to a walk the last hundred yards or so.

Late twenties, he assessed as the details became clearer. No makeup, nice eyes—large and brown. Smallish nose, freckles across it and over her cheeks.

As she seemed to be heading straight at him, he turned around to see what store the phone booth was in front of that had the lady gunning for it with such fierce determination. Promise Hardware. Desperate for a wrench? Just gotta have that Phillips head screwdriver? he wondered and chuckled to himself. This was a lot better than getting pissed off at the phone company.

When he angled his head around again, he was surprised to see that the lady had planted herself in front of him. She was panting slightly, a fine sheen of sweat over her currently ruddy complexion. She stared at him—up at him, actually, as he had nearly a foot of height on her. The expression on her face was both anxious and indecisive as she stood there.

He met her gaze, cocked an eyebrow and waited.

She nibbled on her bottom lip with small, white teeth before speaking. "Excuse me."

"For what?" Marc replied pleasantly.

Just then, the disembodied voice of the phone company lady came on again. "Your call is important to us. Please hold."

Instead of making his blood pressure rise this time, he shrugged it off. Much of life was about waiting, he thought philosophically, and some times were worse than others. Besides, he was curious about the newcomer to the scene.

"Can I help you?" he offered when she failed to inform him of what needed excusing.

Instead she stopped biting the lower lip and ran her tongue over it and the upper one. She had a pretty mouth, he realized. Full, a little pouty, even. Shame to chew on it like that, he thought even as his body reacted in typical male fashion to the sight of a tongue moistening an attractive mouth.

Down boy, he told himself. At this moment, it was obvious that the lady was unaware of her mouth or any effect it might be having on him. She was well and truly upset; there was some kind of war waging inside her. Again, he kept silent. Years of interrogating suspects had taught him that most people hated silence and would rush to fill it up, usually with what needed saying.

Finally, the woman wrinkled her nose and said, apologetically, "It's just that...well...I need that phone."

He nodded, signaling that he was glad to help. "No problem. As soon as I'm done it's yours."

She glanced at her watch, then back up at him. "I need it *now*."

The face was still apologetic, truly sorry to be bothering him, but there was a hint of urgency behind her words that piqued his curiosity. "Why?"

Instead of answering, she said, again, "May I have the phone?"

"Sorry," he said evenly. "No can do." He pointed to the other side of the town square. "There's a whole bank of pay phones right over there."

"It has to be this one." She was insistent now, all apology gone. "It's...really important."

A small spurt of annoyance shot through him; why couldn't anything about this day be easy?

The movers were a day overdue, so after driving non-stop for eighteen hours, he'd had to sleep on the floor last night, and hadn't eaten breakfast yet. He hadn't had a chance to get a cell phone, so he had to use a pay phone to get all the services in his house installed. And now, after he'd been on hold forever, here was this woman demanding to use not just any of several pay phones in the area, but *this* one.

He'd been reasonable so far, but he'd had a disagreeable twenty-four hours and wasn't in the mood for other people's problems.

"Sorry," he said with finality. "This is important, too. I've been on hold forever, and if I hang up now, I'll go to the back of the line." He shrugged, attempted a small smile. "You know how it is."

She nodded, her brown eyes filled with warm understanding for the way life was nowadays. "Yes, I do. I hate being on hold."

"Amen," he said emphatically.

They smiled at each other, and he felt his annoyance fade. If he'd thought her face ordinary, when she smiled it became quite a different thing. There was a kind of glow about her, and her eyes were lit with warmth and humor. She was, he decided, not just attractive, but a *nice* person.

In his former life, he'd run into too few of those. Small towns meant nice people, or so traditional thinking went. He'd see as time went on, but right now, he decided, yes, coming here had been the right move.

"Anyway," he told her reassuringly, "I'll probably be done in five-ten minutes or so. I hope," he added with a small smile.

But her smile left her face. Again, she glanced at her watch. "It's just that I have a time problem."

She wasn't going to give up. Like that, all the good vibes were gone. "I have a time problem, too," he told her flatly. "I'm trying to get my phone at home hooked up, both for personal and professional reasons. It has to be today, it has to be now, and I was here first. Go to another pay phone, okay?"

"No," she said firmly. "I can't."

Two squirrels came bounding out of a nearby tree and tore across the street and into the square, chattering as they did. Neither Marc or the woman paid them any attention.

Removing his shoulder from the side of the phone booth, Marc drew himself up to his full six-foot-three-inches height. Then he gazed down at her and gave her The Look, the fierce, combative expression he'd perfected in fifteen years as a Marine, the last five on assignment with an SIU—Special Investigations Unit.

The Look took no enemies, and had turned ninety-five percent of those who'd challenged him into quivering, apologetic puddles of fear. The other five percent had been whacked out on drugs or too full of testosterone to get the seriousness of the threat to their well-being. Those, Marc had dispatched quickly with a couple of arm twists or tripping. He wasn't a physically violent man unless absolutely forced to be so. He knew his height and build were intimidating, so he didn't press it. Besides, The Look was usually enough.

So, he waited for the woman to quake, to apologize, to back up a step or two. But, amazingly enough, she didn't.

She might have blanched momentarily, but she stayed right where she was, crossed her arms over her chest, and met The Look with a wide-eyed gaze of her own, one that indicated that she continued to feel really, really bad about asking this small thing of him, but wasn't about to back down, not in the least.

Marc was thrown. Sure, his ego was suffering slightly from the fact that The Look seemed to have no effect on her. But he could handle tiny setbacks, had had to do it all his life. No, it was more than that. He had to wonder: Why was the lady pushing this hard? What was going on?

Like that, all self-absorption with his bad day vanished, and he assumed his other persona—investigator. ''I might change my mind,'' he said with a reasonable tone, "but first you have to tell me why you need this particular phone at this particular time."

A veil of secrecy dropped over her expression before she averted her gaze. He felt her retreat, if not physically, then emotionally, before she answered. "It's just that, you see, I'm expecting a call. On this phone." He watched as she fumbled around for a justification. It was obvious that what she was about to tell him wouldn't be the truth.

"Go on," he encouraged.

"It's, uh, my friend. She's in England, and with the time difference, well you know. We, uh, made it for now. Ten o'clock my time, which means, uh…"

"Late afternoon over there."

"Yes, that's right," she agreed happily. "And she's at work. It's her break and if she gets a busy signal—"

"Why don't you cut the crap and tell me the real reason?" he interrupted briskly before she could spin any more fairy tales.

Her mouth snapped shut and she frowned.

Two women walked by, both with short haircuts, one blond, the other dark brown. The latter was pushing an old-fashioned baby carriage. "Hi, Hallie," she said.

Marc watched as the strawberry blonde turned to the two women and smiled distractedly. "Hi, Joannie, Deb," she said with a wave.

The woman pushing the carriage looked pointedly at Marc, then at her again, and raised her eyebrows. "Call me?"

"Later," Hallie replied.

Hallie. Nice name, Marc thought, apropos of nothing, and still curious as the two women went on their way.

The music in his ear changed to the Stones' "Ruby Tuesday," one of his favorites. His head bobbing to the rhythm, he asked, "So, are you going to tell me what's up?" He paused, then added, "Hallie?"

"How do you know my—?" She stopped, then said, "Oh."

"I'm Marc, by the way. With a 'c'"

"Pleased to meet you," she said automatically, in the way of well-brought-up children.

Suddenly her hand shot out and he had the insane feeling she was going to shake it. Instead, she grabbed for the receiver he held. Almost got away with it, too. If he hadn't covered the hook with his free hand, she might have disconnected him.

"Hey!" he said, no longer mellow as he used his elbow to bat her hand away. "What are you, nuts?"

Hallie felt really, truly awful. She didn't want to be doing this, didn't want to take on this giant of a man who had the fiercest eyebrows she'd ever seen, and who had every right to be using this phone.

But the note had said to be at this very pay phone, the one outside Promise Hardware, at ten sharp. So, rights and fierce eyebrows aside, she had no choice.

He was still glaring at her, waiting for an answer. Oh, dear, what to do? she worried. What to do? Lowering her gaze, she was greeted by the sight of a well-used leather briefcase on the sidewalk between his feet. Without thinking, she reached down, grabbed it and hurried away.

"Hey, wait a minute!" she heard the man—Marc—call after her.

Hallie winced at his tone, but didn't stop. This was not the kind of thing she did as a rule, not at all. A law-abiding person with a deep inner moral code of ethics, she knew right from wrong. And this was, without a doubt, wrong. But, as the saying went, desperate situations called for desperate measures.

She continued walking, more quickly now, even when she heard him cursing behind her. Glancing over her shoulder, she saw the moment he left the phone dangling to come charging after her. Quickly, she tossed the briefcase into the alleyway next to Flowers by Flora, watched him change direction to go after it, then she dashed back to the phone, hung it up and kept both hands on the receiver in its cradle, covering the whole phone with her body and praying it would ring before he came back.

The phone was silent. Trembling, she glanced over her shoulder as the man, briefcase in hand, came storming up, his index finger pointed at her, those bushy brows furrowed fiercely and the expression on his face stormy enough to start a war.

"You just messed around with the wrong guy, lady," he growled, then, putting a huge hand on her shoulder, tried to pry her away.

"You must believe me," she grunted, using all the strength she could muster to retain her rights to the receiver, "if it weren't really, really important, I'd never do this."

He yanked again at her shoulder. "I could arrest you for what you've just done."

"Arrest me?"

"Damn right. I'm the law around here."

"You are? Please, you're hurting me."

He snapped his hand back as though from a flame, and she had the sudden insight that he was used to having to watch what his superior strength did to others.

Now he jerked his thumb toward his extremely broad chest. "I'm the new police chief of Promise," he said through clenched teeth.

"Oh. How do you do?"

Even she heard how ludicrous that sounded, but Marc didn't smile. The finger was back, pointing at her again. "I have half a mind to haul you in."

"But, really, I haven't broken any laws, have I?" *Ring, please,* she willed the phone, not sure how long she could fend off the angry new police chief.

"No? You stole my briefcase."

"Not really. I just…moved it. And you got it right back, didn't you?"

Brrrring! The shrill sound made both of them jump a little. Heart racing, Hallie picked up the receiver, held it to her ear and turned her back on the lawman.

"Hallie Fitzgerald?" a muffled male voice said.

"Yes?"

"If you want your stuff back it will cost you."

Behind her, Marc had gone quiet, so she figured he was listening. Keeping her voice as casual as she could, she asked, "Why, what stuff do you mean?"

"Get twenty-five thousand bucks together."

"What?"

"And no police, no FBI, no law, nothing. Got that?"

"I sure do," she said cheerfully, even as her eyes widened in consternation.

It wouldn't do for the caller to know that a representative of the very group of law enforcers she'd been warned against was standing, eavesdropping, inches away.

"Well, now, this is all very interesting," she said lightly into the receiver. "But how do I know—?"

He cut her off. "Twenty-five thousand, I mean it."

"My," she said with a tinkling laugh, "what a lot of money."

"Just get it." With that final pronouncement, the muffled male voice hung up.

Hallie's spirits, which hadn't been too upbeat before, now spiraled even lower. Twenty-five thousand dollars! she thought helplessly.

Slowly, she replaced the receiver on its hook. He might as well be asking for a million. She had no savings, and just made ends meet as it was. And both buildings, the house and the museum, needed a new roof, as well as a bunch of other repairs. Besides, she wasn't even sure the caller had her "stuff," as he'd referred to it. He'd hung up before she could ask for proof.

When a finger tapped her on the shoulder, she jumped and spun around to face Marc. He still looked pretty fierce, but now the look was mixed with curiosity.

For the first time she noticed his eyes. They were

a strange, pale-hazel color, not quite green, not quite gray, nearly opaque, with very thick, very dark lashes that matched those brows and hair. He had a five o'clock shadow at 10:00 a.m., an extremely rugged face, with a sharp nose and a stubborn chin. The short, military-style haircut made his sculpted cheekbones stand out in relief. The man was all angles; there was nothing soft or gentle about him at all.

Which made sense. He was the new police chief. Hallie swallowed down a new spurt of alarm at the realization.

"Well," she said as cheerfully as she could manage, taking the receiver off the hook and handing it to him, "it's all yours."

With that, she walked away, quaking inside, wondering what he'd do now. Would he come charging after her and arrest her? Or would he let it drop? Lord, she'd messed up with that silly story about a call from England. He hadn't bought one bit of it.

Of course he hadn't; she was a terrible liar, always had been. It was her younger cousin Tracy who was the talented fabricator of tales, and Hallie had always wished she'd had a bit more larceny in her nature.

"Hey, you! Hallie!" she heard Marc call from behind her. She stopped and, filled with dread, slowly turned to face him.

"Yes?" she squeaked, sounding like a mouse caught in a trap.

He seemed on the verge of saying something else to her; instead he stared at her a moment longer, then shook his head as though disgusted with himself.

"Nothing," he muttered, but she heard him.

Propping his briefcase against his chest for safety, he inserted money into the pay phone and punched in some numbers. He paid no more attention to her.

Hallie opened her mouth to offer apologies one more time, but snapped it closed again. Although she would love to unburden herself to someone trustworthy, she couldn't explain what had happened, not to this man, especially now that she knew he would be replacing Jack McKinney, still in the hospital after a stroke. "No law," the voice on the phone had said. She would have to figure all this out, somehow, without telling anyone about it.

As she walked dispiritedly back to her house, a wave of sadness washed over her. Oh, how she missed Gram now. Gone a year and Hallie still couldn't get past the ache.

Gram had been her support, her ballast, since Hallie's parents had been killed when she was five. Gramps, too, of course, but he'd been gone for quite a while now. With Gram's death last year, that left only Aunt Julia and her cousin Tracy as family.

Julia was, as usual, somewhere in the world getting her head expanded or shrunk, depending on which kind of guru had The Answer to Life this time, and Tracy had taken off for San Francisco last month and hadn't been heard from since. Just nineteen, she had inherited her mother's wanderlust and willingness to fling herself into new situations without asking questions first. Hallie worried about her ten-years-younger cousin, but then, she always had; the two of them were as night-and-day different as it was possible for cousins to be.

Twenty-five thousand dollars.

The sum hit her again like a sudden blast of cold wind, nearly causing her to lose her balance as panic encroached. How would she find that kind of money? Because, whatever else happened, she had to have her stuff back.

She simply had to.

Chapter Two

"**Y**es, Joannie," Hallie said patiently into the phone as she moved about the living room, "the new police chief, that's who I was talking to, and I'd never met the man in my life before this morning."

"Well," drawled her friend on the other end of the line, "the two of you looked pretty darned cozy."

Before pulling the curtain closed, Hallie took one more look at the street outside. It was such a pretty time of night, still light but fading fast, so that the huge oak trees on the block were outlined by the night sky. The arching, old-fashioned street lamps were just coming on, creating a sense of quiet and order.

If only she could feel that way inside.

"Cozy?" She yanked the curtains shut and moved to the other side of the living room. "Get a new pair of glasses."

"Well, he sure is a hunk," Joannie went on. "Tom says he's an ex-military cop, so everyone's wondering if he's one of those by-the-book, toss-'em-in-the-brig types. Did you get a sense of that?''

"I tell you, I barely spoke to the man."

This conversation was making her uncomfortable, but she concentrated on keeping it light. It was important that her anxiety not transmit itself to Joannie, who had been her friend since kindergarten when Hallie had first come to live with her grandparents in Promise.

And a nicer, more loyal friend no one could have. Yesterday afternoon, when she'd discovered all that was missing from the museum, Joannie had been the first person Hallie had called. Her friend had hurried right over and had spent the entire day with her. Joannie's husband Tom, one of the town's police officers, had even been the one to take the burglary report.

Oh, how Hallie yearned to tell her dear friend about the ransom call, to ask for advice and help. But the anonymous caller had said "no law" and Joannie was constitutionally unable to keep a thing from her husband.

"But you agree, right, about him being a hunk?'' Joannie persisted now. "I mean, you haven't entirely lost your ability to appreciate the male of the species, have you?''

Hallie yanked closed the curtains on the east side of the living room. "Hey, you think he's a hunk. Fine. For me, he's too…large. It's kind of intimidating.''

"Ooh. Large, intimidating. Sounds pretty sexy to me.''

"In a movie maybe. Not in real life."

The anxiety she'd been walking around with all day

was certainly not being helped by this conversation, even though she knew it was Joannie's attempt to take her mind off the stolen treasures. She made herself stand still for a moment, trying to calm her insides. "So, is my goddaughter talking yet?" she asked brightly.

"You're changing the subject."

"We were done with that subject. Answer me."

"If you consider 'da da da,' followed by drool, talking, then I guess she is. Hey, what do you expect from five months?"

"She's perfect. With that darling face, and those fat cheeks, I could just look at her all day."

"She needs more than looking at all day, trust me." Joannie chuckled. "Diapers, baths, spit-up, teething, loading up a bag with enough stuff for a week's stay every time you get into the car with her."

"And you love it."

"Mostly. You'll see, as soon as you have your own."

As soon as. Right. At the rate she was going, Hallie's lifelong wish for a kind husband and lots of kids was looking more and more remote with each passing day.

She moved to the front, north-facing windows, and was about to close the curtains, when her attention was caught by movement on the street. Someone was pulling up at the curb right in front of the house, someone in a dark, mid-sized SUV. She watched as a tall figure got out, slammed the car door, and stepped onto the sidewalk. After checking some papers he was holding, he looked up and gazed at the house. A shock went through her as she recognized him.

"Hallie?" Joannie said on the other side of the line.

"Hmm?"

Oh, God, it was the new police chief. And he was coming up the front walk.

"I just asked if you're sure you're okay, because—"

"I have to go," she interrupted her friend in the middle of a sentence. "Call you tomorrow."

Quickly, she pulled the curtains closed and switched off the lamp, then, shaking her head, switched it back on again. Who was she kidding? she thought as she set the phone into its cradle. It was too late to run around and turn off all the lights, to pretend she wasn't home. Way too late for that.

Why was he here? Maybe he had news about the burglary? Good news or bad? Had he somehow found out about the ransom call?

Instead of knocking right away, Marc took a moment to compose himself. There was something funny going on with his insides, but he couldn't put his finger on just what it was. He took in his surroundings. Porch. Two rocking chairs. Wood flooring, sagging porch roof. A few shingles in need of repair, could use a coat of paint.

He licked his lips. For some reason, his mouth was dry. If he hadn't known himself as well as he did, he would have sworn he was nervous. This was an official visit, he told himself, brow furrowed in consternation as he faced Hallie Fitzgerald's door knocker. Just an official visit. Then why did he not feel his usual sense of being in control?

Exhaustion, most likely. He was wiped out from the drive and the move. Tonight, he ought to be in his new home, unpacking, getting settled in. Instead, he was visiting the victim of a burglary.

This afternoon, a day before the official start of his new job, he'd dropped in to police HQ, had a tour of the two-person jail, met several of his officers, and been shown to his new, ocean-view office. Seated at his desk, he'd leafed through the pile of folders containing open cases and, curious, had opened the top-most one.

It was dated the day before, Sunday, and was a burglary. The victim had entered the premises—some sort of museum—in midafternoon to find many of her valuables missing. There had been no sign of a break-in.

His glance strayed to the top of the form to read the name of the victim: Fitzgerald, Hallie K.

Well, well, well, he'd thought, as the image of a woman with shining hair and a sweet smile flashed before him. Swiveling in his chair, he'd gazed out at the sun-filled vista before him. Well, well, well, for sure.

And so here he was, a few hours later, on her porch. But why, he wasn't exactly sure. His one extremely strange encounter with Hallie Fitzgerald should have been off-putting. Instead he'd been intrigued. Attracted, to be honest. Though he couldn't for the life of him figure out why—she was far from his type.

Still, before coming over to Hallie Fitzgerald's house this evening, he'd actually shaved again. Unusual behavior for him, for sure.

Straighten up, soldier.

The voice came, unbidden, in his head. It had been one of his father's favorite expressions, one he'd heard all his life, from early childhood on, and one that never failed to make him do just that. Stop mind-wandering, dilly-dallying, making excuses. *Stop thinking.* Just get to it, to whatever was in front of him. Take care of it and move on.

So straighten up, he did. Squared his shoulders, stood tall and knocked. He would do what he'd come for, talk to her some about the incident report, and get the hell out of there. Hopefully, she would assume her rightful place as just another statistic, just another victim of a society that increasingly flaunted all rules of conduct and morality.

When she opened the door it was partway only, so Marc was treated to the top of her head. Her hair was pulled back into a ponytail, but wisps of it had escaped and stood straight up, or as straight as curly hair could. She seemed to be staring at his chest, as though expecting a much shorter person. After a moment, her gaze crept upward, reluctantly, he thought, till finally, her eyes met his. They were huge and dark in contrast to the paleness of her face.

He was good at reading expressions but a blind man could have gotten this one; the woman was afraid. Of what? Not him, for sure. She'd shown that by her reaction earlier that day to The Look.

"Ms. Fitzgerald?"

"Yes."

She continued to stare at him, continued to emanate tension and apprehension. He waited for her to ask him in, but no invitation was forthcoming. She remained silent, her eyes wide and watchful.

"Um…It's Marc Walcott, the new police chief. We met earlier today."

"Yes?" It was half an agreement that they had met and half an asking what he wanted.

"May I come in?"

He could have sworn she wanted to say no; instead she gave a reluctant nod and opened the door wider.

As he walked through, his eyes swept the room once and took it all in. It was a small house, and they were in a small living room. Like the outside, it was slightly shabby but friendly-looking. There were amateur landscapes on the walls, two love seats, an easy chair with a faded floral print.

He turned his attention back to Hallie Fitzgerald, who closed the door but kept her gaze focused on him. She reminded him of a family member in a hospital waiting room who knows that what the approaching doctor has to tell her won't be good news.

"Are you all right?" he asked her.

She seemed to consider that one, then said, "Well, that depends, doesn't it."

"On what?"

"On what you have to tell me. I mean, is there bad news or something?"

"Oh. You mean the reason for my visit."

"Yes."

Of course. A cop showing up at someone's front door often meant bad news. He could have kicked himself for not remembering that, but he'd been focused instead on seeing her again and hadn't considered it. If he was aware of a small sense of disappointment that she hadn't been pleased to see him— as opposed to what he represented—he quickly put that away as juvenile and foolish.

"I'm just doing a follow-up on your burglary."

"Follow-up?"

"Yes. I wanted to make sure that everything that could be done was being done."

Man, did that sound lame. The officers who'd filed the report had compiled a complete list of missing items and descriptions, dusted for fingerprints, taken casts of footprints in the surrounding soil, questioned the neighbors. In other words, they'd done their job, and well.

He shouldn't be here at all. As acting chief, his was a mostly administrative job, that of a liaison with the city council, manager and mayor to make sure his department's funding and areas of responsibility were intact and working well. For the most part, individual cases did not come under his purview.

But if they had, there were any number of other open investigations he might have chosen, from a dog-snatching to a hit-and-run of a parked bakery truck to domestic violence—all the fine stuff of small-town life. But he was here tonight because, plainly and simply, he'd wanted to see Hallie Fitzgerald again.

Not a good sign, first day on the job mixing business with pleasure; although, at the moment, there didn't seem to be a hell of a lot of pleasure, not on her part, for sure.

"A follow-up," she said again. "I see."

And like that, she seemed to relax, even offered him a small smile. Which had the effect of drawing his attention to that pretty, pouty mouth of her, those full lips.

"I'm sorry," she said. "Where are my manners? Would you like to sit down? Can I get you some coffee? Cookies?"

There it was again, that second-nature politeness he'd noticed earlier today. It was difficult not to respond in kind. "Actually, coffee sounds great, thanks."

"It'll just take a minute. Come with me while I fix it."

He trailed her into the kitchen, being treated to the rear view of Hallie in faded, coral-colored sweats. The outfit was far from tight-fitting, yet still offered a hint of shapely hips and buttocks beneath.

First he'd noticed the mouth, now the rear. He was thinking like a man, not an officer of the law. This was pure and simple hormones, he told himself, the standard male reaction to several months without a sexual encounter.

Whew, Hallie thought, heading for the coffeepot. A follow-up, that was all. The new chief was here about the museum break-in. This, she could handle, and without having to lie, thank heavens. As long as they stayed on the break-in and didn't get to the phone call.

She put up the coffee and removed several cookies from the pink pig crockery jar. Out of the corner of her eye she noted when the chief sat himself down at the ancient, round, slightly wobbly table that sat directly under the equally ancient overhead light fixture. As he studied the folder he'd brought with him, she couldn't help noticing that his larger-than-life presence seemed to dwarf both the table and the kitchen as a whole.

"I see here a pretty big list of valuables," he said. "Worth a lot of money."

She took down two coffee mugs. "Worth more than money, Chief Walcott."

"Marc is fine."

"Oh. Okay."

"And these were all taken from a different dwelling, not this one. A museum, it says here."

"It's in the rear of the property, what used to be the front in the old days. Shall I take you there?"

"After the coffee. I can really use it. Moving day is tough."

"That's right, you mentioned that this morning. Did, uh, everything work out all right? I mean with the phone company and all?" Now why had she asked that? she chastised herself. Why bring up their previous meeting at all? Foolish, foolish woman.

"Yes."

"Well, good."

She had to forcibly snap her mouth shut before she

apologized for her behavior that morning, but that would have led to the necessity for an explanation, and that would have led to her having to lie again, and that would open up a whole pit of potential problems. Instead she said, "I baked these on Saturday, but they're still fresh."

She set out a platter of oatmeal cookies, noticing the chipped edge of the plate and wishing suddenly that she had one good dish for regular use that wasn't cracked or chipped or mended.

Marc didn't seem to notice. After he took a bite, he nodded as he chewed. "Good. Nothing like home-baked."

Pleased, she took out milk and sugar and set them on the table while he read from his list. "There were several silver pieces stolen, some artwork and books, religious statues, a large tapestry, some antique dolls. It's a good thing you had pictures of everything."

"I had to, for the insurance company."

"And then there's this last item. A scrapbook?"

"Yes, well, it's not just a scrapbook. I mean, it might not have a monetary value, but it's my family stuff. Milk? Sugar?"

"Just black, thanks."

"It's filled with mementos from the past few generations. Pictures, you know, and wedding invitations, birth announcements, a ribbon, a pressed flower. Sentimental value, but very important to me."

As she felt a sudden, totally unexpected sob rising in the back of her throat, she turned her back on the chief and fussed with a sponge, wiping up spilled drops of coffee while she fought to regain her poise.

To Hallie, the contents of her scrapbook were more than just interesting history; they were her roots. Having been orphaned so young, she'd desperately needed a sense of belonging, a *connection* to her heritage. The history of the Fitzgeralds of northern California also included some Vasquezes, Haliburtons, and Rosens, and covered the entire time span from the aboriginal Native Americans to pre-statehood early settlers, from the gold-strike years to the present, from farmland to vacation homes to urbanization. Her scrapbook had been as meaningful to her as a wedding ring passed down from mother to daughter. That missing scrapbook was her lifeline.

Having gathered her composure, she brought two mugs of coffee to the table and seated herself across from Marc. As she did, she was struck by the strangest notion: Having him here, in her kitchen, was oddly comforting. Why, she wasn't sure. He really was so very tall and so very broad, and his eyebrows were so very fierce. Maybe it was the fact that when he was seated, he seemed more...ordinary. Well, not ordinary, but somehow less ferocious.

Then again, maybe he seemed less threatening tonight because he was a man doing his job, as opposed to a man fighting a strange woman for possession of a pay phone.

As she added milk and sugar to her coffee, Hallie watched as he took a sip of his, then nodded approvingly and met her gaze. "Nothing like a good cup of coffee."

One corner of his mouth lifted as he offered the compliment, and she was taken aback by a funny sensation in the pit of her stomach, one that soon spread slowly throughout her bloodstream, bringing warmth to her cheeks. My, oh, my, she thought as she recognized physical attraction, something she hadn't felt for quite a while. Since before her ex-fiancé, Fred, took off a year ago, in fact.

She took a sip of her own coffee before daring to meet his gaze again. Tonight his pale-colored eyes seemed more a calm green than they'd been this morning. She noted the laugh lines radiating out from their edges, and the tanned skin of his face. In the shadow cast by the overhead light, his sharp cheekbones stood out as though they'd been carved from granite. He wore a short-sleeved knit shirt which displayed upper and lower arms thick with muscle and dusted with black hair. He sat tall, his posture erect; the man fairly reeked of self-assurance.

Ex-military. Wasn't that what Joannie had said?

"Yes," he said.

"Yes, what?" Hallie replied, startled.

"I'm ex-military. The Marine Corps, actually. How did you know?"

Oh, dear, she'd said it out loud. She did that sometimes, especially when she was flustered. Thoughts that she was sure she'd kept to herself somehow escaped her brain and made it out her mouth. She'd have to be careful, then; there was a pretty big secret she needed to keep from him.

She shrugged. "Word gets around. My friend's husband is one of your officers. Tom Kingman."

"Oh, yes. I met him today. Good man."

She smiled. "Joannie thinks so, too. So, how long were you in the military?"

"Fifteen years. I got out a month ago."

She wanted to ask why he'd left, but that would be prying, which wasn't polite. She also wanted to ask if his parents were still living and had he ever been married? She had, in fact, a sudden urge to know a lot about the town's new police chief, a lot more than was good for her to know, especially as she intended to keep him at arm's length.

Oh dear, she thought suddenly. Really, the less interaction with this man, the better. Worried, she nibbled on her lower lip. The ransom caller had said no police, but she'd already filed a report, so that part was too late. And, surely, the "no law" thing applied only to the ransom threat, didn't it? Kind of like a kidnapping, where you report your child stolen, but don't let the authorities in on any ransom demand?

Maybe she should just tell Marc to forget the whole thing, to tear up the burglary report. But that would look awfully suspicious. Besides, she didn't yet know if the caller was the one who'd actually stolen her stuff. And if he was, and she couldn't come up with the money or some kind of plan, she'd need all the help she could get from the law before he fenced the treasures and it was too late.

In which case her heart might very well break.

"Ms. Fitzgerald? Hallie?"

"Hmm?"

"You seem distracted. Anything I can help you with?"

Uh-oh, she thought. Busted. Ignoring his invitation

to share a confidence, she took the last sip in her cup, then stood. "Shall I warm your cup for you or do you want to get right to the museum?"

Pretty abrupt, Marc thought, taken aback by her quicksilver change in attitude. Her face, easy to read as a map, had in a matter of seconds registered worry, then sadness, then fear. Whatever she was hiding was pretty major. Was it connected to the burglary? he wondered, or was she wrestling with some completely different, but equally troubling, problem?

For the moment, he would let it rest.

"I guess the museum," he told her.

He followed her to the back door, where she grabbed a large key ring from a nearby hook. Together they exited into the fast-darkening night.

The back porch light revealed an eight-foot hedge all across the yard, with an open archway carved into the middle. When Hallie led him through the opening, he was surprised, and impressed, by the sight of a three-story Victorian home, replete with turrets, steeply raked roof, lots of windows and gingerbread trim. "Wow." He whistled.

"Yes, it's quite something, isn't it?" She gestured with her arm to encompass a vast area. "The surrounding few blocks were part of the original estate. There was the main house, several outlying buildings, gardens and stables, acres of farmland. Over the years, most of the land was sold for development, except my little house and the main one. My grandparents managed to get both of them protected from destruction by having them declared historical landmarks."

"What's left is still pretty impressive."

"If you don't look at the fact that it needs painting and patching and a million other small repairs," she said ruefully, quickly adding, "It's safe. I mean, the ceiling isn't going to come down or anything on the visitors."

"Do you get a lot of them?"

"In the summer, yes. And there're always a few scholars studying early American history, or California heritage, whatever. Come."

Hallie unlocked an ornate wooden door inlaid with panels of etched glass and switched on the lights. As she punched in the alarm code, Marc gazed around the small anteroom which contained an antique desk with several brochures on it, a cash register, and a phone. Various hallways led off from the room into different directions.

"Do you want to see the whole place," Hallie asked him, "or just the areas where the stuff was stolen?"

"It's late. Let's do the short tour tonight, and you tell me what was taken."

There were many rooms, large ones and small, on three floors, and as Hallie led Marc through some of them, his lawman's eye took note of all the valuables contained in them. Several periods in history were represented by costumes, weapons, books, wall hangings and other artwork. There were early photographs of Native Americans, another of an unpaved street filled with horseless carriages. A man with a cigar in his mouth posed proudly in suspenders and shirtsleeves in front of a store. Women at the seashore frolicked in old-fashioned bathing costumes.

After he'd gotten a feel for the place, a quick check of the alarm system showed it to be old-fashioned but serviceable, set to ring at the police station.

"You stated that you set the alarm on the night of the robbery," he said, his gaze raking the anteroom's high windows.

"I always set the alarm."

"But it didn't go off. Who else has access to the keys and the code?"

He noticed that her posture stiffened defensively as she answered. "My aunt, who's in Spain. My cousin, who moved away a couple of months ago. My assistant, a college student named Carrie who is more trustworthy than a saint. And Cal Rankin, who cleans the place twice a week—he's eighty something. Tom already asked me this."

"I know. The cousin who's gone?"

"Tracy?"

"Where'd she go?"

She shrugged. "San Francisco is what she said, but I have no idea for sure. She calls me once in a while to let me know she's okay. I worry, but she's of age."

"Your aunt is her mother?"

"Yes. The apple doesn't fall far from the tree. Aunt Julia takes off, too, but usually to a different continent."

"So then, you're all alone here. No husband, no children, no boarders or tenants?"

"No one."

Marc was pleased to learn this, more pleased than he ought to be. "What about *your* wanderlust?"

She seemed surprised by his question, but considered it before answering. "Don't have much. I'm one of those boring types who loves her hometown and wants to live and die here."

"You're hardly boring."

"Oh, well, thank you."

He looked around and nodded. "It's quite a place. I'd like to come back and get the full tour."

"Wednesday, Saturday and Sunday afternoons, one to five p.m." She grinned. "Five dollars, larger donations accepted."

"One of these days, I'll be here. Come on, it's late."

While they'd been in the museum, night had descended, but as he walked Hallie through the hedge again, a bright, full moon covered everything with a ghostly pale wash. When they got to her back porch, he paused to listen to the sounds of the night. It was quiet, except for the murmur of crickets and rustling leaves. The ocean was several blocks away, so he couldn't hear the waves, but the air was filled with that clean, open, salty smell of the sea.

Gazing up at the moon, Marc thought, not for the first time, that he was glad he'd made the decision to muster out and get a civilian job. A temporary one, to be sure, six months or so at best, which suited him just fine. The town of Promise, situated on the coast near Carmel and Monterey, offered many attractions. Ocean air, sun-filled days, quiet nights. The woman standing next to him.

He inhaled deeply, then let it out. He felt good. More than good. Peaceful.

"Heavenly, isn't it?" Hallie said, also gazing skyward. "Why would anyone want to leave?"

As though a silent signal had been given, they turned to face each other at the same moment and exchanged smiles. Marc gazed at her mouth, her small nose, the wide, pretty eyes. He had the strangest urge to stroke Hallie's cheek, to see if her skin was as soft as it seemed. But he wasn't an impulsive man and he knew his place.

First day in a new town, first day on a new job, cop a feel from a burglary victim? No, he didn't think so.

"Mind if I ask you a question?" he said instead.

"Fire away." Her voice was soft in the moonlight.

"What was the phone call about this morning?"

As he knew it would, the mood evaporated in an instant; the dreamy smile left her face like sunshine going behind a cloud. For a brief moment he regretted asking the question. But he really was here in an official capacity, and he really did have to do his job.

She averted her eyes. "It was…personal."

"But nothing to do with a friend in London?"

She had the grace to grin sheepishly. "No. That was just something I made up."

"If that was an example of lying, by the way, you need to work on it. I'm kind of an expert in interrogation, and you have a collection of some of the biggest giveaways there are. Your face flushes, your eyes get shifty, and you stumble over your words."

An expert in interrogation.

Hallie shivered at the image the phrase conjured up: a small, windowless, airless room, one lightbulb swinging overhead, someone seated in a chair, bound and blindfolded, writhing in agony as a tall, imposing man "interrogated" him.

"You okay?" Marc asked.

She shook her head to remove the picture from it. "I'm fine. And thanks for the hint about the lies. I try always to tell the truth, for just that very reason."

"And the truth this time…?"

Again, she shook her head. "Sorry."

"Anything to do with the burglary?"

She stiffened, but said nothing.

"You might want to let me in on what's going on," he said easily. "I'm a pretty good problem solver."

The man was nothing if not persistent, but there was genuine concern in his question. Even as she told herself to put some distance between them, she couldn't help but recognize, not for the first time, the kindness beneath the gruff, fierce exterior. That part of him warmed her, quite a bit. In fact, just moments ago, she could have sworn he wanted to touch her.

And, lord help her, she'd wanted him to.

"Thanks," she told him. "I think I can manage."

"If you can't, will you ask me to help?"

She cocked her head to one side. "How many ways can I say 'thanks but no thanks'?"

"Probably not enough to push me away. When there's a puzzle, I'm like a dog with a bone. I will chew on it until I get to the marrow." His gaze was steady, steel-like in its determination.

Help. "I guess I'm forewarned then," she said lightly.

"Count on it. Good night. I'll let myself out by the side gate."

She stared at Marc's back as he walked away, musing on this imposing new man who had entered her life, this tall, broad policeman who strode around like he owned the earth. She had a very strong feeling he would not go away.

And, truth to tell, she wasn't sure she wanted him to.

Chapter Three

Hallie set the glass of water down in front of the new customer and without looking at him took out her order book. "Start you with some coffee?" she asked pleasantly.

"If you're making it."

The familiarity of the voice brought her head up with a snap. It was the chief, and he was smiling at her with an easy familiarity. Seven o'clock in the morning and he was clean-shaven, clear-eyed and looked ready to take on the world.

She, on the other hand, knew her lack of sleep the previous night had to be showing and wished suddenly she'd at least put on some makeup, made some effort with her hair. "One coffee coming up," she said, "and no cream or sugar necessary, right?"

"Right."

She went right off to get him a cup, set it down in

front of him and took out her pad again. "Ready to order?"

"Too busy to say good morning?"

Her smile was rueful. "It's been a zoo in here to-day. It seemed everyone had to eat at five o'clock, like maybe if they didn't, the sun wouldn't rise." She inhaled, exhaled, and started over. "Good morning, sir. Welcome to Java. May I have your order?"

He chuckled, then read from the menu. "A stack of pancakes. Three eggs, over easy. Bacon. Tall orange juice. Side order of rye toast."

"Now that's what I call breakfast."

"And I'll finish every last bit of it, promise."

As Hallie scribbled, she was trying to make her brain do its work. Why was Marc here this morning? Did he know she worked the morning shift at Java, or was his showing up a coincidence? No, she corrected herself, of course he knew—he'd had her burglary report with him last night, which had to contain all the information he needed about her job, her schedule. And, as Java was the best breakfast place in town, he would have to show up here sooner or later anyway.

Had he come on purpose…to see her? Or to probe a little more into what she'd avoided talking to him about last night? The man had been in town less than twenty-four hours, she'd seen him three times, and her reaction to him remained the same uncomfortable mixture of pleasure at being with him and dread of what he might find out.

"Okay," she told Marc, "I'll get that order right in."

As she was inserting the ticket onto the rack, Robbie, one of the short-order cooks, glanced over his shoulder and called, "Hey, Hallie, some guy left this for you."

He handed her a crumpled envelope on which her name was printed in block letters. "What guy?" she asked him.

He shrugged. "Never saw him before." Dismissing her, he read the next ticket and turned back to the grill.

She stared at the envelope for a moment, then shoved it into her pocket. Quickly, she served a family of six, topped off coffees, refilled water glasses, pocketed a couple of tips, then looked around and saw that, for the moment, all was clear.

She stepped out the back where another of the cooks was grabbing a quick cigarette, and quickly read the letter. In the same block letters as the original note that had been shoved under her door late Sunday night, were written, "Tuesday. Same phone booth. Same time."

That meant 10:00 a.m. Today. Whoever had sent the letter, whoever had stolen the stuff, had to know that she worked until 9:45. Was it someone from here in town? One of her neighbors? The thought was chilling.

She put the note back into her pocket and returned to the kitchen where Robbie was flipping pancakes. "Tell me more about the guy who gave you the letter, Robbie."

Again, he shrugged. A balding, tattooed, ex-boxer

and recovering alcoholic, Robbie was a man of few words. "Wasn't payin' much attention."

"Tall? Short? Young? Old? Sorry, but it's important."

"You got some secret admirer?" he asked with a wink.

"Tell me."

Sighing, he closed his eyes momentarily, as though trying to form a picture. "White guy. Dark beard. Average height, late twenties, maybe. He had a black baseball cap pulled down over his eyes."

"When was he here?"

"I don't know. Maybe an hour ago?"

"Why didn't you tell me sooner?"

"Hey, Hallie-girl, gimme a break. I'm up to my armpits back here. Which reminds me, here."

The chief's order was up. Balancing all the plates on her arms, she headed for his table.

Marc had been taking in the barnlike atmosphere of Java with interest while waiting for his food. From what he'd been reading about Promise's beginnings, he knew that in the late 1800s, this very room had been a Methodist meeting hall. It retained the same Victorian atmosphere as Hallie's museum, with its wooden floors, wainscoting, wallpaper with a tiny flowered pattern, and cream-colored moldings that ran all around the top of the ten-foot-high ceilings.

Now his attention was drawn to the sight of Hallie walking toward him, plates up and down both arms, and his antennae were quick to pick up the change in her. He sensed an added layer of tension.

Without speaking, she set everything down, went

and got the coffeepot, refilled his and a couple of others, then returned the pot. Back at his table she took out her pad. "Anything else?" She was all business.

"I may need dessert."

Despite her preoccupation, her eyes widened. "Wow, you really do have a healthy appetite, don't you?"

"I burn it off pretty easily."

He watched her face—a nice, pretty, clean face, he thought, with that sprinkling of freckles—and was pleased to see the slight flush that came over her cheeks. Was her picture of him burning off calories anything like his?

"I'll check back with you later," she said quickly.

Her attitude was cordial at best. On guard. It was as if the moonlit moment on her back porch had never happened. Frowning, he watched her walk away, then went to work on his food. He had other matters to attend to than Hallie Fitzgerald and her problems. This was his first official day as chief of police. A long day stretched ahead of him, beginning with a meeting with his entire staff at eight sharp.

This time when the pay phone rang, Hallie was right there and didn't have to fight anyone for it. "Hello?"

The same muffled male voice answered her. "How're we doing on that twenty-five thousand?"

"We're not. And listen, I want proof that you have what was taken."

"Proof, huh? Well, let's see," he drawled. "Right

now I'm holding a real old doll. She has this long, frilly, yellow and white dress on. Sound familiar?'' There was a noise like someone going through a box. ''Here's some itty bitty spoons and a big hat with a feather in it. And, oh yeah, there's this real ugly scrapbook. Lots of ratty old pictures in it. Maybe I'll just take it and the doll and the spoons and just throw them all into the city dump—''

''Okay, okay,'' Hallie interrupted, her heart in her throat. The doll was early Victorian, over a hundred and twenty years old. And the scrapbook, the one she'd told Marc about last evening…if anything happened to it, she would die.

''I believe you. But, please, I'm not a rich woman. I have no idea how to get my hands on that kind of money.''

''Don't you?'' he drawled again. ''Think about it.''

She did, and like that, she got it.

Tracy's trust fund. It contained exactly twenty-five thousand dollars. Hallie was the trustee, until Tracy's twenty-fifth birthday.

How did he know about…?

''Tracy!'' she said, sudden anger at herself replacing the fear. How could she have been so stupid, so naive? ''Is Tracy there?'' she snapped at the man on the other end of the line.

''What Tracy is that?''

''You tell my cousin that this is not the way to get her hands on the money. You tell her that she's given me a fright that I'll never forgive her for. You tell her she'd better call me at home tonight.''

"Or what? You'll go to the cops? You do that, and all your little treasures here? They're history."

At his words, fear came back with a vengeance, and Hallie had to swallow it down before she could speak again. "Just tell her," she said, less belligerently now, "to call me tonight. After I talk to her, then we'll see about your twenty-five thousand. Do we have a deal?"

But he'd already hung up.

Feeling equal parts furious and helpless, Hallie strode quickly back home. How dare Tracy do this to her? Nineteen and as irresponsible as a ten-year-old.

She'd wanted that money the minute she'd turned eighteen, but Hallie had followed Gram's wishes—not a penny until Tracy was twenty-five and, it was devoutly hoped, had a little more sense. That was what the will had said, and Hallie had been determined to honor it.

What would she do now? Would she give her flighty younger cousin the money in exchange for the return of all the stolen property? And who was this man Tracy had obviously hooked up with? Sure, her cousin's taste had always run to bad boys of one sort or another, but, as far as Hallie knew, not criminals. What had she gotten herself into?

Tonight. Tracy would call her tonight, and the two of them would talk. Hallie had rescued her cousin from scrapes most of her life. Somehow, Hallie told herself, determination in her step, they'd get this thing worked out.

They just had to.

* * *

Overall, Marc thought as he walked the three blocks over to Java the next morning, he was adjusting pretty well to his new life. The police department was so well organized that taking the reins was easy. There would be a few personality problems, but nothing he couldn't handle. When the town's manager, Len Baker—an old Marine buddy of Marc's—had offered him the job, he'd told him that there might be some resentment from two of his captains, Coe and Johnson, each of whom thought the job ought to have gone to him. At the meeting yesterday, Marc had been prepared for a figurative pissing contest, but, for the present, at least, both men had seemed willing to cooperate. Probably, he figured, because he wouldn't be around that long, so they were biding their time.

The morning air was crisp and he breathed it in with pleasure. Promise was one hell of a find. Sure there were the usual disputes between the progress-at-any-cost and the change-over-my-dead-body groups. There was crime, but not a lot. Teenagers acted out, but nothing serious had to be addressed.

There were several churches of varied denominations—not surprising, considering the place had been founded as a religious summer retreat—their congregations devoted. Marc wasn't much of a believer himself, but he'd observed that strong ties to the church seemed to do more good than bad, and that families which consisted of a mother and father tended to have the best, most leveling influence on kids.

Not that you'd know it from him. He'd had both, sure, but his father laid down the rules and roared when they weren't followed, while his mother seemed to fade a little more each year until, by the time Marc was twelve and his brother six, she was dead. He'd never known she'd been ill all that time because he'd been so busy busting his ass to please his dad, he hadn't asked.

Most of Marc's memories of his mother were of pale, lifeless eyes and boniness, a silent woman who served them meals, washed their clothes and nodded. It wasn't until much later on that Marc realized how damaged the family dynamic had been; as a child he accepted the pecking order without question: Dad, Marc, Stevie, then Mom.

Consequently, he'd had his share of affairs, with a variety of women, but he still tended to prefer the company of other men. It was tough getting a handle on members of the fair sex—they seemed to operate under a different set of rules. A confirmed bachelor, he knew that he had too much of his dad in him; it was a constant battle not to try to control his surroundings with an iron fist.

As he turned the corner onto Pacific Street and smelled that wonderful fresh coffee aroma emanating from Java, he smiled all over again. What a find. Terrific, fresh food and unbelievable coffee. Not to mention that one of the waitresses on the morning shift was none other than Hallie Fitzgerald.

She intrigued him. She turned him on. And he still couldn't figure out why. She was pretty enough and her body was trim and evenly proportioned, but she didn't wear low-cut clothing or exude sensuality. What she exuded was good health and a mostly sunny nature.

Except...

He frowned as he pulled open the door to the restaurant, only to have his senses assaulted with more delicious odors—bacon, coffee, toast, fresh muffins, all at the same time—making him nearly light-headed with pleasure.

Except, he mused again, making his way to the same table he'd sat at yesterday, the woman had a secret, and it was one that was tearing her up inside. He wanted to help, as the law if necessary, as a friend if that was what she needed.

Why the word "friend" came up in his thoughts, he had no idea. Marc had never been friends with a woman in his life. Sex always got in the way. Men were friends. Women were, well, women.

Seated at the window, with a full view of the street, he waited. Sure enough, Hallie came up to him, this time with a cup of coffee in one hand and a glass of water in the other. She offered a smile of greeting, but it didn't make it to her eyes, which had even darker circles under them than yesterday, and yesterday's had been pretty dark.

"Good morning, Chief," she said, pulling her pad from her pocket. "What's it going to be today?"

"Are you okay?"

"Fine."

"Pardon me for saying it, but you don't look fine. Is it the burglary? I was swamped yesterday, but I'll check on the progress this morning when I—"

"I didn't ask you about that," she snapped, then seemed to catch herself. In a more pleasant tone, she said, "Your order?"

She was so uncomfortable with him, she was practically squirming, but he gave it one last shot. "Hey, Hallie, remember I told you I can help?"

"You can help by giving me your order," she said brusquely. "I have a lot of other customers to wait on."

The way she said it was like a slap, and he felt himself recoil. His first instinct was to retaliate, but, instead, he focused his attention on the menu. "I'll try the oatmeal today," he said coldly, "with raisins and brown sugar, side order of sausage, tall orange juice."

"Less than yesterday, I see." Her tone was conciliatory, which meant she was trying to make up for snapping at him.

But he wasn't having any of it.

He'd done his best, and it just proved what he'd known all along. Women were a different species, and you couldn't be friends with them.

As she changed out of her waitress uniform, Hallie couldn't contain the edginess that skittered up and down her nerve endings. Once again, she glanced at the phone in her bedroom, willing it to ring. But it remained, as it had last night, silent.

Tracy hadn't called then, did not seem to be calling now, and Hallie was worried. Her cousin was often a pain in the butt and drove her to tear her hair out sometimes, but she loved the younger woman, and knew Tracy loved her.

Hallie stepped into the shower and let the hot, soothing water wash all over her. She tried to make

her mind a blank so she could enjoy the sheer sensual
pleasure a shower always brought, but her mind had
a mind of its own. Something about this whole deal
didn't make sense. Hallie was certain Tracy and her
twenty-five thousand was behind the robbery; she just
knew it in her gut. So, she'd told the man on the
phone that after she talked to her cousin she'd be
willing to discuss the money.

Why hadn't she called?

What if Hallie's gut was wrong and her operating
assumption was incorrect? The caller hadn't confirmed the connection with Tracy, had only sneered
and remained superior.

She turned off the water and toweled herself dry,
her body clean but her mind racing. As she applied
her museum makeup and did her hair, she couldn't
stop the questions from arising: Who had robbed the
museum? Where was her cousin? What if she were
ill? Or dead?

Hallie heard herself moaning and knew she'd let
her imagination run wild. She was strung tighter than
a wire. She had to get hold of herself, *had* to relax.

She rotated her head, slowly, so as not to disrupt
the carefully arranged hairdo. It was all part of the
look, part of the service she offered on Wednesday,
Saturday and Sunday afternoons. She gave a guided
tour of the museum, and the visitors deserved her
best. It was Wednesday, and she was due to open in—
she glanced at the clock—fifteen minutes! By then,
she had to appear as normal as possible.

Marc plunked down his five dollars, even though
he knew as the chief he could have gotten in free.

But he was on his lunch hour, his own time, and felt better about paying his own way. The plump and pretty young woman who took his money told him the next tour was in ten minutes.

As he waited, he thought about this morning's encounter with Hallie. Sure, he'd been hurt by her behavior, but later on, he'd decided to be generous and let it go. It wasn't her nature to be rude, and whatever pressure she was under was making her act out of character. He was just going to have to insist, he figured, that she let him in on what was troubling her.

His attention was caught by an old, framed needlepoint to the right of the reception desk. It read: When this you see, remember me. It was signed, Beatrice, 1887.

He found himself smiling at the thought of a proper young Victorian girl, bent over her stitchery and unaware that someone well over a hundred years later would read her message. Was she one of the Fitzgerald ancestors? he wondered, and as he did, Marc was, quite suddenly, overcome with a feeling he could only describe as nostalgia for a past he'd never experienced.

Which was odd. He wasn't given much to sentimentality, didn't consider human history as worthy of much thought except as it taught the same lesson over and over again: people were both savage and striving not to be, and whichever instinct won out determined the direction of their lives.

He was interrupted in his musings by the sound of conversation right behind him, so he turned around.

Hallie was talking to three visitors, a middle-aged couple and an earnest young student type who was scribbling away in a notebook. But his quick observation of them lasted only seconds because his gaze was riveted by Hallie.

His eyes widened. This wasn't the Hallie of the waitress uniform and ponytail, nor the after-hours Hallie in sweats. For one thing, her hair was most definitely not flyaway today. It was swept up on her head in some sort of intricate coil thing and decorated with two fancy combs. Dainty pearl earrings dangled from her lobes, and a long line of pearl buttons ran down her high-necked blouse. Lace decorated her wrists, and she wore a dark-blue, ankle-length skirt and high button shoes. All these details he took in quickly, but it was the whole picture, the *shape* of her in this outfit, that made him catch his breath.

Her breasts were high, her waistline tapered in dramatically, then flared out again at her hips. Wow, he thought quietly. And wow again. Old-timers had told him that a buttoned-up woman was way sexier than one who wore revealing clothing, but he'd never bought it. Give him flesh and lots of it, he'd always said. Leave imagination to the poets.

But, man, he got it today. Hallie, with her hourglass figure and nary an inch of skin showing except for her face and hands, had been transformed into a woman of mystery. And grace. Not to mention unconscious sensuality.

Marc was taken aback by the fierce pounding in his loins as he gazed at her, a desire so strong that he turned back to the needlepoint for a moment to catch his breath and give his body time to return to resting position.

He shook his head. What was it about this woman? Why did she keep surprising him? Why did she keep having such an intense effect on him? He didn't like surprises, so part of him didn't care for the sensation in the least. However, another part was jumping with joy, willing to go along for the ride and see just where it took him.

Right this minute, it was taking him on a museum tour, with the Victorian lady as his guide.

"Miss Hortense Palmer, my great-great-great aunt, who was to become Promise's first female mayor, came to town in 1884. She purchased five lots, extending from Silver Avenue to Pacific Street." Hallie pointed to a painting of a stern-faced woman, dressed plainly in dark blouse, long skirt and boots and sitting in a room that seemed surprisingly dainty, considering the fact that she held a six-shooter on her lap.

"Shortly after moving," she went on, "Hortense became annoyed at the chickens and horses who used her property to congregate. She asked the animals' owners to keep them fenced in but was ignored. She built a six-foot wire fence, which kept the horses out, but didn't faze the chickens, who flew to the top and crowed down at her, victorious."

The members of her small tour, consisting of Marc and four others, chuckled appreciatively. She always liked telling this story, but today found herself directing it mostly at the chief, performing for him, really, as there was no mistaking the appreciation in his eyes every time hers locked with his. It felt good to be admired, she had to admit. It had been such a long time.

In the past half hour, as she'd pointed out the Native American basketry, the details of a dormer window, the doll collection of Eleanor Anne Beasely, who had died of diphtheria at age ten, Hallie had felt Marc watching her with a disconcerting intensity.

At first, her cheeks had reddened with embarrassment; eventually, another element joined the embarrassment. Beneath her corsets, she felt her breasts respond and knew that her blouse must have revealed it. The warm sensation in her stomach had made its way down to a more intimate area. All this had been, needless to say, distracting, and had threatened to disrupt her duties. It was all she could do to keep her attention focused on her lecture.

"Hortense asked for permission to shoot the chickens, which was given because no one thought she was serious. So, she got herself a gun—" Hallie pointed to the one in the painting "—and did just that. Shot two of them and tossed them over the fence."

"Oh, no," gasped a bespectacled young woman.

"They were going to be slaughtered anyway," Hallie said with an understanding smile, "so Miss Hortense, as she was known all her life, just quickened their end. When the chickens' owners made a fuss, it turned out that a lot of town members were glad she'd done it, as their yards were also being invaded. A new resolution was passed, prohibiting the running at large of chickens and other domestic fowl in the town of Promise. Miss Hortense was a heroine.

She was much revered, although feared, too, and went down in legend as the gun-toting, chicken-shooting, lady mayor of Promise. She never married and died at the age of ninety-one.''

''My, how interesting,'' chirped an elderly lady, and her equally elderly husband nodded.

''Thanks. And that about wraps up our tour, ladies and gentlemen. Feel free to wander about,'' Hallie told them with a gesture encompassing the other rooms, ''but please don't touch anything. Many of these objects are very old and extremely fragile.''

Her tour members dispersed to various exhibits, except for Marc. Smiling, he walked over to her and stood very close. ''So, that's your aunt, huh? Tough old lady.''

''That she was.''

His gaze took a moment to tour her entire face before he said, ''If she never married, how are you related?''

This close, those magnetic eyes of his seemed to probe deeply into her soul. ''She had a brother and a sister,'' she said in a voice that came out breathlessly, ''both a lot younger than her, and they moved with her to Promise. I'm descended from the brother's line.''

''You keep track of all that, huh? Ancestors, all that stuff? Genealogy?''

''I sure do. It's kind of my hobby.''

He offered a small half smile and lowered his lids a bit. ''Any other hobbies?''

A perfectly innocent question, Hallie knew, but

there was a suggestiveness to it that made her want to fan herself. "Well, I, uh—"

Whatever else she might have said was lost in the ringing of Marc's cell phone. Scowling, he pulled it from his pocket and put it to his ear. "Yeah?... Okay, I'll be right there." He flipped the phone closed and returned it to his pocket. "Gotta go. Sorry."

And with that, he was gone.

She told herself she ought to be relieved, as he was such a distraction. Instead, it felt as though a light had been turned off, some source of heat and energy removed, and she felt not just chilled but alone.

"Run along, Carrie," Hallie told her student assistant. "It's nearly five and no one else is coming. I'll close up."

The plump young woman looked up from sorting the brochures on the reception table. "Are you sure, Hallie?"

"Hey, you have a final tomorrow, right? Of course I'm sure."

With a grateful "Thanks *so* much." Carrie hurried away. Hallie went up the stairs to the second floor to make sure all the lights were out. Once there, her attention was drawn to a photo hanging by the switch, one that truly had no value to anyone but her. It showed a nice-looking young couple dressed in classic 1970s style—she had on a long, filmy dress, he wore bellbottoms and a T-shirt and had hair to his shoulders. The woman held an infant daughter, dressed in a matching dress with a large bow in her very short hair. The man looked down on the baby with adoration in his eyes.

As Hallie gazed at this picture of a happy, loving trio, she felt tears forming. Whoever had robbed the place had taken most of her family mementos, but they'd left this behind, thank God. So now there was only this one picture of Hallie and the parents she barely remembered. Five was too young to have many memories, but she knew, deep inside, that she'd been wanted and cherished.

As she was alone up here, she allowed the tears to fall freely. She didn't hear the footsteps on the stairs until a cough behind her made her turn suddenly.

Marc stood at the head of the staircase. The smile left his face as soon as he saw her tear-stained face, and he rushed over to her, alarm in his expression. "Are you all right, Hallie? What is it?"

"It's nothing," she tried to say, swiping at the tears. But more of them appeared, making her sniffle.

"Hallie," he said, grasping her upper arms and pulling her to him, wrapping his muscular arms around her and holding her close. He was so big! she thought. And strong. He smelled good, like clean sweat and warm sunshine, and she let herself rest against his massive chest, experiencing a feeling of safety so overwhelming that it made her cry some more.

He patted her hair. "Did something bad happen?"

She shook her head silently, then looked up at him to tell him it was just her emotions, nothing more. But the moment her eyes locked on his, an involuntary gasp escaped her. A connection sizzled between them, like a fuse lit from both ends. She felt it from her toes to the top of her head, and knew, without a doubt, that he felt it, too.

As she gazed at him, his nostrils flared, and desire, strong and hot, flashed in his eyes, matching the same sensations that were making her skin burn with need. The hand on the back of her head became firmer. His arm moved down to her waist and pulled her even closer.

Transfixed by the fire in his eyes, she watched as his mouth descended to meet hers.

Chapter Four

His mouth was strong, his lips soft, and she met his kiss with an eagerness that took her by surprise. Fred had never tasted this good, she thought, as she drank from Marc like a woman deprived of water for far too long. A sound issued from his chest that was part groan, part growl, and she sighed and sank into him even more, shivery sensation after shivery sensation pounding through her bloodstream.

When she felt his tongue pushing its way into her mouth, she parted her lips to greet it with her own. He pulled her more tightly to him till there was no air between them. Their bodies met like two parts of a whole, and she wanted only to drown in the sensation and never come up for air.

What are you doing? asked a small, inner voice.

Go away, Hallie answered silently. *I'm enjoying this.*

Again the voice intruded, more insistent now. *Are*

you crazy? This is the one man whose arms you shouldn't be in, the man who can make big trouble for your family.

That last warning, the one about her family, registered, big time. Quickly, she broke the kiss, pushed herself away from Marc and his embrace, and backed up a couple of steps. Unable to face him, she studied the floor, her face aflame. "That shouldn't have happened."

"No?"

"No."

"Why?"

She forced herself to raise her head and meet his gaze. Chin jutted out, she tried to think of how to answer him. Before she could, he took a step toward her, reached out and pushed a wayward tendril of her hair, one that had come loose during their kiss, behind her ear. That one, light touch of his fingertip around the top of her ear made her vibrate all over again.

She swallowed down her reaction. "I'm not interested."

"In what?" he murmured, pushing again on the loose strands that refused to stay put. His eyes, those strange, pale hazel orbs, were gazing at her hair with a concentration that was so focused, it might be the most important task of his day.

"In…uh…anything physical."

"Coulda fooled me."

Slowly, languorously, his gaze moved over her flushed cheeks, past her chin and neck, and came to rest on her breasts, where she knew her hardened nipples were outlined against the soft fabric of her blouse.

He offered a knowing half smile. "Funny how these prim, old-fashioned clothes reveal so much."

Hallie had to resist the urge to cross her arms over the telltale signs of arousal, but felt the flush deepening on her neck, felt her cheeks burning. Marc knew just how to disconcert her. All she had to do was to meet his gaze and she was toast.

The only way to break the spell was to turn and walk away from him, so she did just that. As she straightened a small wall hanging that hadn't been crooked in the first place, she said, "Aren't you on duty or something?"

"I'm pretty much on twenty-four-hour duty," she heard him answer from behind. "That's my job."

Not one to take a hint, he came up behind her; even without being able to see him, she could feel his body's heat on her back. Again, he touched the traitorous tendril of hair, but this time he curled it around his finger.

"But I'm also the boss," he murmured in her ear, his breath warm on her skin, "which means I can pretty much come and go as I please."

With shaking fingers—he really unnerved her!—Hallie pushed his hand away and took off again, this time heading down the stairs. "At any rate, I'm going to forget that happened."

He followed right behind. "Why?"

"You always ask so many questions."

"And you always avoid them."

At the bottom of the staircase, she turned to face

him, clasping her hands under her chin, begging him. "Please, Marc. I don't know how else to say this so you understand."

"Try the truth."

"It is the truth: I'm saying no. That's spelled N—O."

From his position on the last step, Marc realized he towered over Hallie even more than usual, and probably appeared threatening. But this conversation they were having wasn't putting him in the mood to make her comfortable. Her face, as she looked up at him, was a smorgasbord of emotions. Pleading, fear, frustration. The remnants of desire, too, no doubt about it.

"You're saying no to what?" he asked gruffly. "Kissing you? Asking questions? Being concerned about you?"

"Yes."

"Which?"

"All of them."

Quickly, she turned and walked down the short hallway toward the reception room. He followed. Once there, she pulled open the front door, letting in the fading, late afternoon, autumn sunshine, and there she stood, like a sentinel, pointedly inviting him to be gone.

Dammit, he thought clenching his fists, aware that he was in imminent danger of blowing up at her. The woman was impossible! "All right then," he said, and walked through the doorway, leaving Hallie behind him. Then, unable to stop himself, he turned and added, "Remember the dog with the bone? I'm out of here...for now."

He noted with satisfaction that his not-too-subtle warning made her blanch slightly before she closed the door on him. As he walked away, he told himself not to be put out that she'd basically thrown him out of the place. Hallie Fitzgerald, he was pretty sure, was more at war with herself than with him.

And she was most definitely as turned on by him as he was by her; he'd known it the minute he'd tasted her mouth, had seen the evidence in her body's reactions to him. Oh, yeah, it was mutual as hell.

But the man—woman chemistry they shared did nothing to solve the mystery of what she was keeping from him. Between beginning a new job and feeling in a sexual fog of desire, he hadn't been thinking clearly. That had to stop.

As he approached his vehicle, he put his mind to work. From the beginning, she'd acted strangely. Her puzzling behavior at the phone booth had occurred the day after the burglary. The two had to be connected. She'd mentioned "a lot of money," he remembered. Had she been the one to stage the robbery? For insurance purposes?

It was obvious Hallie needed money; not only did the house need repairs, but she worked way too hard—five mornings at Java, an afternoon and both weekend days at the museum. No days off, barely any hours to herself. Maybe she just thought it was time to get a little of her own back. Take a trip, buy a new car. Robberies had been staged for less.

Nah, he thought, starting the car. His instincts rebelled at the idea of Hallie masterminding anything illegal. She was basically law-abiding. But whenever he got close, she sure got shifty on him. And he'd been wrong before.

In his first year in Special Investigations, there had been this baby-faced kid, freckles, blue eyes, a bright, innocent smile, the front tooth chipped. Everyone had loved him, and as he'd enlisted straight off an Iowa farm, they'd all called him Homer. It was a while before anyone discovered that he'd been dealing cocaine to the troops for months. Marc had been the one to crack the case, and only sheer coincidence—of being in the latrine during a buy—had made him happen on the truth.

So, lesson learned: Appearances meant nothing.

Still, he thought as he drove away, in his heart, he was pretty sure Hallie wasn't involved in ripping off her family treasures. There was too much pain associated with their loss, and he'd bet the bank it was genuine.

He wished he had more time to devote to this, but the week had been taken up with personnel problems, scheduling, educating himself and meetings with the town's muckamucks. As soon as he could, he would get to the bottom of Hallie Fitzgerald and her secret. He could be a patient man, when called for. And when the prize was worth winning.

Marc showed up at breakfast on the next two mornings, making sure to be seated at her station, so even if she wanted to, Hallie found she couldn't avoid him. To his credit, he kept their conversations light and nonintrusive, and always brought paperwork with him that seemed to take most of his attention in between bites.

Which was good, because Hallie wasn't happy with the confused, conflicted feelings he aroused in her.

"So, what's with you and the lawman?" asked Java's owner, Meg Delaney, from her position behind the reception booth.

"Nothing," she told her friend and employer.

Meg, tall and with red hair a shade or two darker than her own, propped a fist on her hip. "Who are you kidding?"

"I mean it, Meg," Hallie insisted, loading up a tray with dishes to be bussed. "He's new in town and he's lonely. We're friends, that's all."

When Meg glanced at the new chief Hallie followed her gaze. Marc was watching her intently—there was nothing casual about it—and she quickly turned her attention back to the tray.

"On your part, maybe," Meg said dryly. "I'll be following the progress of this 'friendship,' but my money's on the cop."

Hallie had more on her mind than Meg's observations. She hadn't heard from the man on the phone again. Nor from Tracy. She'd called all her cousin's friends, but no one knew where she was. Hallie was nearly out of her mind with worry.

The sound of the phone on Saturday morning woke her from a deep sleep, one she'd needed badly. She'd been restless, tossing and turning for nights now, so she'd taken a mild sleeping pill.

"Hello?" she said, groggy.

"Hallie?"

"Hmm?"

"This is Marc."

She sat straight up in bed, as though he'd just entered the room and she didn't want to seem at a disadvantage. "Hi."

"Did I wake you?"

"It's okay."

"I have some news on your case."

Her heart rate increased. "What news?"

"You know we've circulated a list of items stolen from the museum?"

"Yes?"

"We just got a call from Santa Cruz that a pair of candlesticks that strongly resemble yours were brought into a pawnshop there. Willing to identify them?"

"Of course. When?"

"I'll pick you up in a half hour."

"You're going? Not one of your officers?"

"It's a nice day for a drive."

After throwing the covers off the bed, Hallie ran down to the kitchen and put on coffee. Then she called Carrie and asked her to open the museum. Santa Cruz was about a half hour up the coast, depending on traffic; she'd probably make it back, she told Carrie, near to opening.

Candlesticks, she thought, her mind still fuzzy from the pill. Was it good or bad that they'd shown up? And should she hope that they were from the museum, or that they weren't?

By the time Marc picked her up, she was showered

and dressed. She'd even put on a little blush and mascara, telling herself that she'd have to rush into her costume later on, and this was a good way to get a head start on it. The fact that she would be alone in a car with Marc, the man who sent her pulse into overdrive every time she saw him, she pushed away from the front of her brain.

It really wouldn't do to dwell on an attraction to someone she needed to keep at arm's length. It really wouldn't do at all.

"I'm honored," she said as she settled into Marc's SUV. "The police chief himself is tracking down stolen property."

Busted, Marc thought. She was correct—by all rights, one of his officers should be making this trip. But he'd taken it on because he wanted to see her reaction to the candlesticks. And, dammit, he wanted to be with her, alone, away from prying eyes, not in the restaurant.

"I figured it was a good way to see some of the coastline," he said easily, which seemed to satisfy her.

As he drove them away from Hallie's place, he noticed how she gazed around the interior of his vehicle. "Mmm, this is nice. It has that new-car smell. Is it?"

"Yup."

"Leather interior, too," she said wistfully, moving her hand over the soft material.

"Nothing but the best," he said lightly. "I've had used cars my whole life, so I decided this time to get a new one."

"One of these days," she said with a sigh, "I'd like to say the same thing. Steve down at the garage has told me that soon he's not going to be able to put my trusty old Toyota back together again. I don't know what I'll do then."

"It can be tough coming up with money for a new car."

"The toughest."

They headed north on Highway One. On the left, the ocean sparkled under clear skies, but darker clouds gathered over the mountains on their right. "It's supposed to rain later," he said.

"Yes, I know. I don't expect too many visitors to the museum. Tourist season's about over and the weather makes it worse." For a while, she stared straight ahead, as though deep in thought. Then she turned to him, a frown between her brows.

"Are you sure these are the missing candlesticks?"

"Ninety percent sure."

"But there's a chance they're not?" she asked, and it was impossible to ignore the edginess beneath the question.

"Yes."

Strange, he thought. She almost seemed to want them not to be the missing items. Which was puzzling. Wouldn't you want to get back possessions that had been stolen? Which led his thoughts back to the robbery-for-insurance money theory again, even though he didn't want to go there.

By unspoken mutual agreement, they kept the conversation on general topics, the weather, the scenery. It turned out Hallie liked basketball a lot, baseball some, and cared not a whit for football; his preferences went the other way. He had four years of college, courtesy of the military, and she had two. His mother was dead, his dad lived in Florida. They both liked to read, voted every year but for different parties, and agreed that *The Godfather* was the best American film ever made.

The pawnshop was located in the downtown section of Santa Cruz, a coastal city that boasted a large University of California campus in the hills above the town proper and a long fishing pier with a popular amusement park on the adjacent boardwalk. The population was equal parts students and old-timers, with a generous sprinkling of ex-hippies who hadn't yet decided to adapt to the twenty-first century.

The moment Marc identified himself and his mission, the shop's owner, a Vietnamese immigrant only too pleased to obey the law of his newly adopted country, quickly brought out the candlesticks.

Hallie took one look at them and gasped. Her face registered sheer terror as she blurted out, "Oh, my God! He's selling them!"

"Who is?" Marc asked her.

A millisecond went by before she replied, "Whoever it is that stole the stuff," but it was just long enough to confirm his suspicion—Hallie knew who had robbed the museum.

Damn, he thought with a sinking heart. "Sure he's selling them," he said caustically. "That's why people steal valuables, to fence them. Why are you surprised?"

"Well...I guess, I've never had this happen before."

Another lie, badly told. Another attempt to cover up for something she wished she hadn't revealed. They just kept mounting up and up. What he ought to do was take her in for questioning, but have someone else do it. He was too involved, emotionally. He knew it and was really unhappy with himself.

He turned to the shop's owner. "Who brought these in?"

In stilted, but excellent, English, he told them it had been a young-ish man, Caucasian, skinny, with a beard, and a blue or black baseball cap. He'd told the shopkeeper that the candlesticks were a family heirloom, and there had been no reason to doubt him. It was only later when the shop's owner had looked at the list of stolen items that he'd made the connection. It had happened on Thursday.

When Marc asked if there was anything else he could tell him, the shopkeeper replied, "Only that after he left, I heard the sound of a small truck or a van. Either it was his or someone else's." He shrugged. "I'm not sure."

Out of the corner of his eye, Marc had been keeping track of Hallie's reactions, and at the moment she was looking at the candlesticks with the saddest expression on her face. "Know any skinny young men with beards?" he asked her.

His question seemed to startle her, but she glanced over at him with a rueful expression on her face. "About a hundred. This is northern California."

"Any who have a van?"

"Probably, but none that I can think of." She shook her head, adding, "Right off the bat, anyway." She was telling the truth, for once, he could tell. But what else was she keeping from him?

Hallie's mind was working furiously, trying to make sense of everything. How could Tracy do this? The family heirlooms were sacrosanct, not for sale at any price! Hallie had never thought Tracy capable of this kind of mischief, one that would inflict pain on the family, most especially on Hallie.

Marc had the candlesticks tucked up under his arm as they made their way to the car, his strides purposeful. She had to hurry to keep up with him.

At the car door, he turned abruptly. "Dammit," he said, his eyes flashing, "tell me, and tell me now. What do you know about this?"

His words had a ferociousness behind them that made her back away from him. "Nothing," she lied, hating herself.

He grabbed her upper arm with his free hand, hurting her with his strength. "Don't, Hallie," he said through gritted teeth. "I know there's something."

As she pulled her arm away from his grip, and rubbed it, she saw the dismay in his eyes. Just as she'd observed him do another time, he fought to keep his temper and succeeded. As upset as she was, there was a part of her that had to admire the man for his control. Someone with his superior strength could inflict real damage.

He walked around to the passenger door, yanked it open and barked, "Get in."

Feeling somewhat like a naughty child, she did as

she was told. By the time they were both settled into their seats, she could tell Marc had regained at least some of his composure. Without starting the car, he turned to her, his left arm looped over the steering wheel.

"Tell me what you're hiding."

When she didn't answer, he said, "I ask you this because I'm worried about you, okay? I know you're involved in this thing somehow. If I had any sense I'd haul you in for questioning."

That one took her by surprise. "What?"

"You're guilty about something. For all I know, you could have had a part in planning the robbery, for a start."

Filled with indignation, she glared at him. "I had nothing to do with it! How could you think such a thing?"

He didn't back down. "How could I not?"

Raising his right hand, he ticked off the points on his fingers. "One, you're one of the few who had access to the museum, its keys and security code. Two, you claim not to have heard any cars behind your house on Saturday night or Sunday morning, but you could be covering up. Three, the day after the burglary, you receive a mysterious phone call, not at your home, where it might be traced, but at a pay phone. That call could easily have been from one of your associates. Four, every time I ask you about it, you clam up and invent some stupid story that wouldn't fool anyone. And five, just now you said 'He's selling them,' like you know who 'he' is, but then deny you do right after."

He threw up both hands in disgust. "Hey, maybe you have a male accomplice. You could have planned it, he could have executed it. There you'll be, counting your insurance money, while we look like amateurs."

Hallie's jaw fell open in dismay. She was shocked, to her very core, by Marc's accusations. And hurt, too. Deeply hurt.

"But—" She had to swallow once before going on. "But none of that is true. I swear on my parents' grave."

"Then what was the phone call about?" he shot back.

Her mind was racing. She felt absolutely awful to have Marc think so badly of her...although, to be fair, she could see how her evasiveness must look from his perspective. Oh, how she yearned to enlighten him. She owed him an explanation. He'd been so patient.

Could she tell him? Days had gone by without a phone call from the unknown man, who, it appeared, was selling her treasures. There was no deal with him, if there ever had been.

Was it okay now, finally?

Can I tell Marc the truth?

"Yes," he said, "you can."

Oh, lord. She'd done it again, said it aloud. But maybe it was for the best. There was no backing out now.

Her mind made up, she looked him right in the eye and said, "Okay. It was a ransom call."

"A what?"

She reached out and placed a hand on Marc's arm. It was thick with muscle, contracted with tension. "But you have to believe me. I knew nothing about the robbery beforehand and have no idea where the stuff is or who stole it. The whole thing came out of nowhere and took me by surprise."

For several long moments, he stared at her, assessing whether or not she was telling the truth. Then he nodded, and she knew he did. A great weight lifted off her shoulders and flew up into the air.

"Go on," Marc said. "The ransom call."

"The day after the burglary, I got a call from a mysterious man telling me if I paid him twenty-five thousand dollars, I could have the stuff back. But if I told the police, he'd get rid of it." When Marc nodded again, she continued. "He called again on Tuesday to see if I had the money. I asked for proof. You know, how did I know he actually had my things? And then he described an antique doll and I knew he did."

And then I told him Tracy had to call me that night.

Hallie bit her lip before she let that one escape. No, she couldn't go there. She had to keep Tracy out of it until she knew just how involved her cousin was in this.

Instead, she withdrew her hand from his arm, leaned back against the closed door and rubbed her eyes tiredly. "I don't know what happened. He just hung up. I haven't heard from him since." She shrugged. "And now here are the candlesticks and I don't know what's going on."

Again, his gaze roamed her face, but not with the

previous suspicion. This time, she saw concern there, and she felt a twist of conscience in the pit of her stomach. She'd told the truth, but she'd left something out, something pretty important.

But there'd been no choice.

"So, that's why you didn't tell me what happened," he murmured as he turned the key in the ignition. The powerful engine roared to life.

"Yes. I was afraid I'd never see my things again. I wanted to tell you, you must believe me."

"You didn't recognize the voice?"

"No."

"How did he communicate with you?"

"By note. And no, I didn't keep either one. I wish I had."

"Either one?"

"He must have slipped the first one under the door Sunday night, I guess. I found it Monday morning. I was to be at the pay phone in front of Promise Hardware at ten sharp."

"I remember," Marc said ruefully.

"I imagine you do. And he dropped off the second one at work on Wednesday. Same place, same time, it said."

He threw her a sharp look. "You saw him?"

"No. Robbie, the cook, he saw him. From what Robbie told me, he sounds a lot like the man who sold the candlesticks back there." She pointed to the pawnshop.

"Okay, now we're getting somewhere."

With the engine running, Marc flipped open his cell phone and called in instructions to have both Robbie

and the pawnbroker work with a composite artist, and
to have both of them look through the books of
known felons. When he got back, he'd have some
candlesticks that needed to be checked for fingerprints.

Hallie watched him, admiring the way he took
charge with a mixture of assurance and diplomacy.
She wondered where he'd learned this skill. It didn't
go along with the image she held of rough and tum-
ble, testosterone-packed, fighting Marines. But then,
most of her pictures had been formed by movies, so
what did she know?

He flipped the phone closed, pulled out of the parking space and headed out of town. "The notes, did
you throw them out?"

"Yes, but garbage day was yesterday, so they're
gone."

Marc nodded, but his mind was working on the
new information Hallie's confession had given him.
Man, was he relieved. He knew now, for sure, that
she'd had nothing to do with ripping herself off, and
his mood was so buoyant, that he felt about a hundred
pounds lighter and twenty years younger.

"I wonder why he hasn't contacted you again," he
speculated out loud. He didn't expect an answer from
Hallie and didn't get one.

The minute they hit Highway One, he noticed that
the dark clouds were rolling in quickly. He glanced
at his watch. "Let's grab some lunch."

"I can't," Hallie said. "I have to get back."

"You also have to eat. I've only known you a
week, but it seems to me you've lost weight." He

handed her his cell phone. "Call someone else to open the museum."

"But I'm the only one who gives tours."

"What happens if you get sick?"

"I don't get sick."

"But what if you do?"

She shrugged. "Then, they read the brochures and wander around by themselves."

"Works for me."

When she offered no response, he sighed. "Look, sit with me while I have lunch, all right? I'm starving."

"What else is new?" Hallie said with a small laugh, then called Carrie.

Chapter Five

Fog rolled in with such amazing speed, that within seconds, Marc was unable to see in front of him. "So, this is the famous northern California weather, huh? You could bump into a tree and not know it."

When he was able to make out a sign pointing to a restaurant to their right, he turned in that direction. Carefully, he steered the SUV up a narrow, winding road, and pulled into a small parking lot, then he and Hallie dashed into the restaurant, before the rain got them. Once inside, both of them stopped and gazed in wonder at the fantastic scene set out before them.

The round, high-ceilinged restaurant was all windows, rising twenty or so feet upwards. On a clear day, you could probably see the ocean, but today, with nothing but fog outside, the whole building felt like an aerie surrounded by plumes of gray-white clouds.

A polished wooden floor contained various booths,

all of them works of art—thin metal shapes of green and gray, curved for two, with thick cushions.

"I guess fast food is out," Marc said, filled with awe.

"It looks expensive," Hallie whispered.

"Well, what the hell. Game?"

Without waiting for an answer, he allowed the host to steer them to one of the window booths. Hallie was seated near the window, Marc right next to her. He ordered them hot coffee, large bowls of soup, and bread. To start.

The rain had hit with full force by now so huge drops pounded against the windows. A furious wind accompanied the rain, each gust making the windows rattle. They sipped hot coffee and silently gazed out at the storm.

After a while, Hallie angled her head around and, eyes shining, said, "This is like a fairy tale. Like we've dropped out of reality and into another world. Do you agree?"

She smiled and waited for him to comment, but he could only smile back and say nothing. Through a trick of the light, her face reflected the raindrops falling outside, and the sight mesmerized him.

Now that he knew she was innocent of any crime, he was free to loosen the leash he'd been holding on his feelings for her, and he was swept with a whole bunch of them as he gazed at her. There was a warm sensation, deep in his gut. An overpowering desire to protect her, to take on all her troubles and make them his own. But not in a paternal way.

Because what he felt for her had nothing to do with being her daddy.

"Marc?"

"Hmm?"

"You're staring at me."

"That's because you're beautiful."

She wrinkled her nose. "I am not, but thanks for saying it."

He couldn't resist playing with her hair; from the first, it had fascinated him. "May I ask you a question, a personal one?"

She went still, slightly on guard. "I…guess so."

"The day I came upon you, after the museum tour, you were crying. Why?"

He felt her body relax. "I was looking at a picture of me and my folks. They're gone. They died in a car accident when I was very young. I was raised by my grandparents, and sometimes…" She stopped, and he could tell she was fighting some strong emotion.

He stopped fiddling with her hair and put his hand on hers, cupped it in his larger, stronger one. "Go on."

"Not to sound dramatic, but sometimes I feel the weight of the world on my shoulders. You know, all the responsibility for the museum and the house and the family heritage. And I wish they—my folks— were still here." She gave an embarrassed shrug. "I'm a little too old to be needing Mommy and Daddy, but there you are."

He squeezed her hand. "I don't think we're ever too old to need comfort."

Hallie met Marc's intense gaze and saw in it all

the inner strength of the man. A feeling of such security, such *safety,* came over her that all she wanted
was to crawl up inside him and be held. Being with
Marc was like leaning against the trunk of an old tree,
knowing it had been there forever and would be there
forever, and never having to worry about it falling
down or being demolished.

She'd never felt safe like this with Fred. Never.
She'd enjoyed her ex-fiancé's company, liked being
part of a twosome, but always she'd kept part of herself back from him, maintained her separateness.

"Who comforts you?" she asked Marc.

Her question seemed to take him by surprise.
"Me?"

"Yes."

A frown formed between his formidable eyebrows.
"I don't need comforting."

"Never?" When he shrugged, she smiled. "Is this
a guy thing? Real men don't admit need?"

He seemed to consider her question. "Maybe. If I
feel needy, I go for a run or get a beer, distract myself.
Women and men are different, in case you didn't
know."

"I think maybe in the way we deal with things, we
are. But I think all human beings, whatever their gen-
der, have the same emotions."

"Do you?"

"Yes."

Once again he squeezed her hand. His nostrils
flared slightly as he murmured, "I feel lots of emotions when I'm with you."

She caught her breath, and she could swear she

could hear her heart pounding in her chest. "Do you?"

He nodded, his gaze roaming her face. "And I can't tell you how glad I am that you finally told me everything. Do you feel better now? I do."

The corner of his mouth quirked up as he said that, but Hallie's stomach took a dive in the opposite direction.

"Yes," she said, and it was at least partly the truth, "I feel a lot better."

Something warm and soft was rubbing her cheek and she raised a shoulder to capture the warm thing and make it stay.

"Hallie," a deep male voice said. "Wake up. We're home."

"Huh?"

Her eyes popped open and, disoriented, she looked around her. She was in Marc's car and he was smiling at her. His hand—the soft, warm thing that had been rubbing her cheek—rested on her shoulder now, massaging it lightly. They were parked in front of her house.

She ran a hand over her face and licked her dry mouth. "I must have fallen asleep."

"Pretty much the minute we left the restaurant. Looks like you needed it."

Her hand flew to cover her mouth. "Oh, God, did I drool or anything?"

He chuckled. "Nope. You just slept and looked too peaceful to disturb."

"Well, thanks." She inhaled, then let it out. "You're right. I did need that."

"So it seems." He swiped a finger across her cheek one last time, then before she could protest, he'd opened his car door, hopped out and came around to open hers.

"You shouldn't have," she said. "You'll get wet."

"Real men don't mind getting wet," he said with a smile. "There's an umbrella somewhere. Shall I get it for you?" Soft raindrops pelted his thick black hair and ran down his face, but he seemed totally unperturbed.

"Nope. I love the rain." She stepped out onto the curb and, closing her eyes, held her face up to the sky. The drops of moisture felt good after her deep sleep. "What a terrific lunch. Thanks."

"My pleasure. We'd better get you inside or you'll get soaked. Come on."

He took her arm and hurried her up the path to her house. On the porch, they faced each other. She didn't really want to say goodbye to him, and she had the feeling he felt the same.

Marc made a face. "I have to go. I want to get those candlesticks into the lab right away. But I'll see you tonight."

"Tonight? Oh, heavens, I'd almost forgotten."

"Good thing I reminded you, then. The invitation said you were one of the hosts."

"Well, yes, but I don't *do* anything there. Just show up. All the descendants of the founding families are hosts. So you'll be there?"

"At the one hundred-twentieth birthday celebration

of the founding of the town of Promise? Wouldn't miss it for the world. Promise you'll save a dance or two for me.''

She felt strangely shy at his casually tossed-off request. Pleased, too. ''Well, sure, okay. I'll see you, then. Thanks again,'' she added one more time, then opened the door, waved once, and closed it behind her.

The phone was ringing as she entered and she grabbed it. ''Hello?''

''Hallie?''

''Tracy? Are you okay?''

Her cousin burst into tears, but managed to say, ''Yes.''

Hallie sank into the armchair near the phone table, her churning emotions a mixture of relief and anger. ''I've been so worried about you. Where are you? Sure you're all right?''

''Yes,'' she said, sniffling, ''except for being stupid.''

''It was you behind the robbery, right?''

''No. Well, not really. Well, kind of. I mean—'' she sniffed again ''—I told this guy about the money and how I wanted it and how angry I was at you for not letting me have it, and he said why don't we take a few things to teach her a lesson, and then you'd give me my money, and well, it seemed like a good idea at the time.''

Hallie's heart sank. A good idea at the time. To cause her stress and worry, to just about break her heart.

As though reading her cousin's mind, Tracy said

timidly, ''But, Hallie, I know I was wrong. I mean, I'm so sorry. I don't know what came over me, I was just so resentful at being treated like a child who couldn't handle her own money.''

''And then you did something really mature like rob your own family museum.''

''Oh, Hallie,'' Tracy said, crying again. ''I hate myself.''

Ordinarily Hallie soothed her younger cousin when she was having one of her down-on-herself spells. But not today. Her own hurt went too deep to play the role of comforter. Sighing, she leaned back in the chair.

''At least you're all right. But who's your accomplice?''

''Just some guy,'' Tracy answered vaguely.

''Just some guy? What, a stranger? Someone you met in a bar?''

''No, no, of course not. He is…was…is my boyfriend.''

''What's his name?''

''You don't need to know that,'' she said shiftily. ''Anyway, everything will be all right, I promise. We'll be returning everything we took.''

''Are you sure?''

''Absolutely,'' Tracy said with conviction.

''Because cousin Fay's candlesticks showed up in Santa Cruz today.''

''Well, yeah, but that won't happen again, I promise.''

Tracy and her promises. She always meant them at the time, but didn't always follow through. ''When?''

"When what?"

"When are you bringing the stuff back?"

"Real soon. Don't worry, okay?" With that final recommendation, she hung up.

"Tracy?" Hallie said into the receiver, but they'd been disconnected. Quickly, she punched in *69, but whatever phone number Tracy had called from was blocked.

Don't worry. Right, she thought. She had no idea where her cousin was, or when the stolen items would be returned, but she was not to worry. She shook her head at the girl's total lack of regard, or sense of responsibility, or compassion for someone else's feelings.

But, Hallie told herself, at least she was alive, not lying in some ditch, dead. Her cousin had a lot of growing up to do and Hallie hoped both of them would survive it.

Marc was impressed by the preparations that had been made for the birthday celebration. Playa de Amor—a large, tree-filled grassy knoll that jutted out into the bay, and which bore a pretty risqué name for a town with such conservative roots—had been tented over for the occasion. The wet grass from the day's rain had been covered with tarps and plywood. A full buffet table stretched the length of one side of the tent, there was a bar in one corner and a small combo playing oldies rock in another. Several candlelit tables encircled a dance area.

He was greeted the moment he came in by Len Baker, the town manager, whose once-lean physique had succumbed to a softer life. Marc was quickly introduced to Len's wife, Fran, a pretty woman with a face too young for her salt-and-pepper hair.

Len shook Marc's hand enthusiastically. "How're you settling in, Captain? Or should I call you Chief?"

"Marc, please, Len. I'm a civilian now. And things are okay. Chief McKinney set up a great system, so I'm just stepping in. How is he, by the way?"

Len shrugged. "It's slow recovering from a stroke, but he's a tough old bird. Any problems with Coe and Johnson?" he asked, naming the two captains who had been passed over in favor of Marc.

"Nothing overt. And nothing I can't handle."

Len slapped him on the back. "Talk about tough old birds."

The town manager turned and gazed with pleasure at the people who'd attended. "Funny, both of us here, in management positions. Long way from the mud and mosquitoes on Guam, huh?" He turned to his wife. "Did I ever tell you how Marc here rescued me and three others from a swamp during training exercises?"

"Yes," she said patiently. "A time or twenty."

"Rescue, bull," Marc protested. "I tossed you a rope."

"And pulled four grown men out like we were sacks of grass cuttings."

"Put it down to adrenaline, okay? And leave it at that."

As he finished his sentence, his attention was caught by a vision in pale pink who stood near the buffet table.

Len followed his gaze. "There's our Hallie Fitzgerald. You've met, I take it?"

"My favorite waitress."

"Real shame about that break-in. Any progress?"

"We recovered a pair of candlesticks today. We'll
get him, whoever he is. Please excuse me."

Hallie was checking on the food, making sure everything was going well. Contrary to what she'd told
Marc earlier, she was more than just a hostess; she
was one of a three-person committee who had put this
whole thing together. The moment she'd returned
from the drive to Santa Cruz, right after Tracy's call,
she'd been on the phone making sure all the plans
were being carried out.

The good news was she hadn't had to cook, or hang
decorations—all her work had been in planning. Tonight all she had to do was show up and look pre-
sentable.

She was wearing the same spaghetti-strap, floor-
length, pink silk dress she'd worn as Joannie's maid
of honor four years earlier, the gown that she wore
every time formal or dressy wear was called for. One
of these days, she told herself, she'd get something
new, maybe not pink—which was a bit on the girlish
side for a woman fast approaching thirty. Maybe this
time she'd get something shocking and sexy. She was
tired of looking wholesome.

As she waved to someone she knew, she noticed
Marc across the room and that she was the object of
his intense gaze. Which didn't make her feel wholesome, not in the least. This man brought out an ex-

tremely sensual side to her nature, awakened needs that hadn't been addressed in a long time.

She'd recognized it the time they'd kissed, maybe even before that, if she were honest with herself. And she'd felt it earlier today, over lunch in that magical restaurant high above the trees and among the very clouds themselves. He'd been the one to say it out loud, to be quite clear that he had feelings for her. But she hadn't responded.

Whatever fierce desire she felt for Marc had not, up to now, been welcome. Always there was that incipient threat to her family. Although…

She reconsidered as she watched him make his way toward her. She'd told him about the ransom. And if what Tracy said was true, if all the stolen goods were on their way back, then the police would no longer have to be involved, and she would no longer have to protect her cousin.

Her cousin. The ungrateful, immature idiot! Sudden anger surged through her. Maybe she should tell Marc the whole thing and let the girl suffer the consequences.

But no, that would be putting him in an awkward position. Telling a lawman that a robbery wasn't really a robbery and her cousin wasn't really a thief—what would he do with that information? What could he do? He'd have to act on it, especially as chief of police.

No, better to keep quiet about it, see if Tracy returned the goods. If she didn't…

Stop it! she told her furiously racing mind as Marc came up to her with a smile. Relax. Just for tonight, how about she let herself have fun, put her worries, all of them, out of her mind? Money, new roof, old car, stolen goods, worry about her cousin, the mourning period for Gram, the rejection by Fred—all of it. She would let it float away for one night.

Mind made up, Hallie smiled back at Marc, a buzz of excitement in her tummy area as she gazed at him. He looked, well, gorgeous, in his dark blue suit, cream-colored shirt and matching tie. It was perfectly tailored to accommodate his ridiculously broad shoulders and height. She loved to see a man in a suit.

The casual California lifestyle made it a rare sight, so she was especially pleased to see Marc in all his glory. With his clean-shaven visage and those sculpted cheekbones, she knew that if she had the slightest amount of artistic talent, she would want to draw him.

Her three-inch heels meant that as he stood before her, she didn't have to crane her neck quite so far back to meet his appreciative gaze.

"Good evening," he said with a slight bow of his head.

"Good evening," she said back, tamping down the strangest urge to curtsy. For a brief moment, she felt like someone out of one of her ancestors' time. They could be at a fancy-dress ball, she would be holding a fan. A suitor might approach her, bow from the waist as she curtsied, eyes downcast modestly.

Except the look in Marc's eyes tonight tossed modesty out the window. "You look lovely," he said.

"Do I?" She shook her head, ruefully. "Thank

you, but I was just thinking that I needed a new dress.''

''It's new to me.''

''I guess that counts for something, doesn't it?'' she said with a smile. ''And while we're on the subject, your suit is scrumptious.''

He cocked one dark eyebrow. ''Scrumptious?''

''Probably not quite the right word, huh?'' She felt warmth in her cheeks. Not just the suit, but the entire man looked good enough to eat....

No, she thought, don't go there.

''It's…really well tailored.''

''This is the first time I'm wearing it. I've been in dress blues for this type of occasion for years.''

''Well, it looks like it was made for you.''

''It was. I had to go to a tailor. I'm not really built for off-the-rack.''

''No, I imagine you're not. You're so, I don't know, broad. Muscular. Not too muscular, I mean, not like one of those body-building magazine guys or anything.'' More heat gathered in her cheeks. Getting in deeper and deeper, Hallie, she thought. Smiling ruefully, she said, ''Uh, maybe we should stop discussing your body now.''

One half of his extremely attractive mouth turned up slightly. ''We can discuss yours if you'd like.''

''No, I don't think so.''

''Then how about we dance instead?'' he said, as the combo began to play ''My Funny Valentine.''

The moment she went into his arms, the sensation of being there felt right. Familiar. And, again, safe. All her body's tensions and worries evaporated. His embrace was strong but solid rather than threatening, and he danced surprisingly well for such a big man. He led her expertly around the dance floor, joining other couples so inspired.

Hallie closed her eyes, rested her head against his chest, and sighed. As she felt his muscular thighs pressing against her, she felt more alive, more alert—and yet more peaceful—than she'd been in a long, long time.

This feels so good.

"Yes, it does," Marc whispered in her ear.

She'd said it out loud. But that was okay. It did feel good. More than good. Absolutely, totally lovely. Snuggling even closer, she let herself float.

"Hallie?" Marc whispered again in her ear.

"Hmm?"

"The band stopped playing, and they're taking a break."

"Huh?"

She raised her cheek from his chest and looked around. Sure enough, they were the only two left on the dance floor. The musicians' instruments were on their chairs, but nary a musician in sight.

"Oops," she said. "I guess I went away there."

"Where to?" He led her to the side, keeping hold of her hand as he did.

"I have no idea, but it was really nice."

"It was like that on the drive back today. You looked so peaceful sleeping there in the car, I hated to disturb you." He frowned. "Should I be insulted that you fall asleep when you're with me?"

"Just the opposite. Take it as a compliment."

The Silhouette Reader Service™ — Here's how it works:

If offer card is missing write to: The Silhouette Reader Service, 3010 Walden Ave., P.O. Box 1867, Buffalo, NY 14240-1867

NO POSTAGE
NECESSARY
IF MAILED
IN THE
UNITED STATES

BUSINESS REPLY MAIL

FIRST-CLASS MAIL   PERMIT NO. 717-003   BUFFALO, NY

POSTAGE WILL BE PAID BY ADDRESSEE

SILHOUETTE READER SERVICE
3010 WALDEN AVE
PO BOX 1867
BUFFALO NY 14240-9952

"Compliment accepted." He lifted the hand he still held and kissed her knuckles lightly. Her skin tingled where his mouth had touched it.

It was such a courtly gesture; again, she had a flash of being in an earlier time, when there was a strict code of conduct, courtship rituals. There was something of the old-fashioned gentleman in Marc. Sure, he was tough and modern, but he also opened car doors, took her elbow when they walked. His manners were excellent.

The dichotomy was really quite attractive. Heck, everything about the man was attractive, and now that she'd decided she could let that feeling flower, see where it led, it seemed to be galloping along much more quickly than she'd imagined.

"I'm starving," he said. "Shall we go to the buffet table?"

"After that huge lunch? If I remember correctly, you not only had soup, but a salad, a sandwich and chocolate mousse."

"Metabolism. Can't help it. Feed me or I get really bad-tempered."

"Well, heavens, we need to avoid that, don't we?"

"Hallie!"

Joannie came up to them, pulling her tall, prematurely balding husband Tom after her. After she hugged Hallie, she turned eagerly to Marc and held out her hand. "You must be the new chief," she said with a broad, bubbly smile. "I'm Joannie Kingman, Tom's wife."

With a smile, Marc shook her hand, then nodded to Tom, who looked decidedly uncomfortable, but re-

signed. Joannie had an exuberant personality, always
had and always would. Tom had learned long ago to
get used to it. He adored her and she adored him, and
Hallie thought it was one of the best marriages she'd
ever seen.

Joannie put her hand through her husband's bent
elbow. "Tom says you're doing great this first week.
Everyone's quite impressed."

"Joannie," Tom said warningly, shaking his head.

"Well, what's wrong if I tell him that?"

"Because he's the chief, and isn't interested in
what I tell you over the kitchen table."

"Actually, I am, Tom," Marc said. "I welcome
feedback."

Tom shuffled his feet. "Yeah, well…"

"Tom says even Bennett Coe and Larry Johnson
aren't giving you any trouble, which is really interesting, since they can't stand each other and both
wanted your job."

"Enough, Joannie," Tom said. "No more department business, okay? Or I'm dragging you out of
here, and we wasted a perfectly good baby-sitter."

"Joannie." Hallie grabbed her friend's hand and
pulled her away. "Let's let these two talk shop a little. I need a glass of wine. Thanks for the dance,
Marc. See you."

She whisked her blond, overly talkative friend to
the bar, Joannie complaining all the while. "What did
I say? It was all complimentary to the chief."

"Poor Tom," Hallie said. "Such a straight-arrow
kind of man to have such a loose cannon like you in
his life."

They were joined at the bar by Meg Delaney, Hallie's boss, and the three women sipped some wine and gazed around the room. There were over a hundred and fifty townspeople there, everyone decked out in their best finery.

"When do we start the speeches?" Meg asked. "I want to make sure I'm out of here by then."

Hallie laughed. "We're keeping them short this year, promise. By the way, the buffet table looks great, Meg."

The tall redhead looked pleased. "Manuel and Ivan did it all. Have you two tasted the blinis yet? To *die* for."

"I had a huge lunch today. Maybe later."

"And I just got here," Joannie said, then elbowed Meg in the ribs lightly. "Look at her," she said, referring to Hallie.

"Yup," Meg replied. "Can't take her eyes off him."

Hallie turned to find both her friends gazing at her with mischievous expressions. "What?"

"The chief," Joannie said with triumph. "The two of you are perfect together."

Not for the first time that evening, Hallie blushed. "Will you stop it? We danced once, that's all."

Meg snorted. "You call that dancing? Looked like a pre-mating ritual to me. And you haven't engaged in one of those since nasty ol' Fred ran off. You're falling hard, girl. Fess up."

Hallie made a rueful face. "Okay, I'm attracted to him. I mean, how could I not be? Look at the man."

The three women did just that, focused their gazes

on Marc as he and Tom talked. His back was to them, but just at that moment, as though some secret radar had informed him of Hallie's position in the room, Marc pivoted and faced them, nodding his head in their direction.

"Caught in the act," Meg said with a laugh.

Joannie waved and declared, "I was looking at my darling husband, I'll thank you to know."

Hallie felt Marc's eyes lock on hers, and almost swayed from the power they exerted over her. She barely heard her friends' chatter. All movement in the room seemed to come to a stop, all its light and energy suddenly focused on two people, Hallie and Marc, alone in the universe for a moment in time.

"Hallie," Joannie said, nudging her elbow. "You might want to put your tongue back in your mouth. You know? Play a little hard-to-get?"

"Too late," Meg pronounced. "The woman's a goner. And so is the man."

Her two friends watched as Marc nodded to Tom, then strode toward them. Hallie had to suppress the silliest giggle of joy at seeing him.

Oh boy, she thought, *I am falling and falling hard.*

And all signs pointed to the fact that the feeling was, most definitely, mutual.

Which was, most definitely, a great way to begin.

Chapter Six

For Marc, the next two hours passed in a blur of new faces, music, delicious food...and Hallie. She was different tonight, freer somehow. She was charming and funny and sweet, and he wanted to spend the entire evening with her, but, of course, that wasn't possible. Too many other people needed to welcome him to town.

He was introduced to so many people, he found himself asking forgiveness in advance if he forgot names. He met most of the major merchants, the school principals, the two priests and several ministers. Everyone beamed when he and Hallie danced; between dances, others entertained him with stories of her childhood, her eagerness to volunteer when others were in need. He'd been impressed with her sunniness before; now he understood where it came from. She was loved, deeply loved, by the townspeople, and had many close, lifelong friends. She thrived here, where her roots were.

He couldn't escape a fleeting regret that his own life had been so nomadic, first with the childhood of a military brat, and then his own years of service with postings in all parts of the world. How would it have been, he found himself wondering, if he'd had a real home, a real sense of belonging? If the majority of people he'd interacted with had been "normal"— whatever that meant anymore—and he hadn't been the type of man who was attracted to the military way of life?

But he was who he was and so, as always, he observed it all through the eyes of an outsider.

He heard speeches, joined in the applause, was introduced from the podium, hardly necessary as he'd shaken the hands of everyone there. And, whenever he could, he returned to Hallie, to dance with her, to talk and joke with, to admire. As the evening wore on, he wanted more.

About eleven, when some of the older folks were heading out, he deliberately waltzed her through the tent's back flap and up the shallow steps of a large, white, latticework gazebo that perched at the edge of the cliff.

Once there, under the domed roof, he gave in to the urge he'd had to ignore all evening: He kissed her. Eagerly, hungrily, at first. Then he put the brakes on and really explored that pouty mouth of hers. It became a long, drawn-out kiss, unhurried and exciting as hell.

Desire fogged his brain, but eventually he realized

that Hallie was trembling, and he broke the kiss. "Are you cold?"

"Only when you let me go."

He removed his jacket and put it over her shoulders, then pulled her to him again. "I'm not letting you go."

"Good."

"And," he added with a smile, "I'm really glad you're not telling me to stop this time."

"Are you kidding? Don't you dare. Stop, I mean."

He drew her over to one of the gazebo's stone benches, sat down, and pulled her onto his lap. Cupping her face in his hand, he kissed her again. She groaned and cuddled closer. His body tightened with sexual tension and he told himself to take it slow, take it easy. Anything that felt this good was worth taking time with.

"Hallie," he murmured, "you taste so good." He kissed her eyes, her soft cheeks, moved his mouth down to her neck. She arched back to grant him more access, and now it was his turn to groan. There was no way, sitting as she was on his lap, that she could miss his rock-hard response to her body.

Beyond the gazebo, people were saying goodnight, calling out to each other with the amiability of lifelong friendships. Vaguely, Marc was aware of other sounds—the gentle lapping of waves against the rocks, a sea lion's plaintive roar.

But his senses were filled with Hallie. He kissed the gentle swell at the top of her breasts, then cupped one small, firm mound in his hand. Her hands tightened on the back of his head as she squirmed under his touch. She was so responsive, he thought, so willing. It was all he could do to take this slowly, and he wondered if it would kill him.

He ran his thumb lightly over the hardened nipple that stood out against the silk of her dress and heard her quick, indrawn breath of desire, one that matched his own.

"If we're not careful," he murmured, his mouth filled with the sweetness of her skin, "we could disgrace ourselves right here."

"That wouldn't do, would it?" she murmured, pressing his hand more tightly to her breast. "A member of one of the founding families and the chief of police? Bad move."

He shifted his mouth to her ear and ran his tongue over its whorls. "How about later?" he breathed. "I could take you home."

"I have my car here."

"I'll meet you there. Say yes."

He heard her swallow. An agonizing moment went by while he waited. "Yes," she whispered finally. "I have to stay for another half hour or so."

"I'll be by at midnight."

As though of one mind, they stood and kissed once more. Together they walked back to the party, not touching, and not needing to. There were still some social matters to attend to.

Later, they would have all the time in the world.

For the first time in her life, Hallie understood the expression "all a-twitter," because that was just how she felt inside. She stood in the middle of the living room, totally up in the air about what to do next. She'd fluffed the pillows on the couch, turned on the lamp, the one with the pretty antique shade that stood by the fireplace, and made sure there was no dust on the coffee table.

What now? she asked herself, then ran upstairs, kicked off her three-inch heels and sighed with relief. Barefoot, she smoothed out her bed, turned down the covers. Then she pulled them up again. Too obvious.

A nervous wreck, that's what she was. Also aroused, almost senseless with need. Also scared to death, not sure what she was getting into. It was all going so fast. From a plan of a little flirtation all the way to welcoming Marc to her bed. In one night. She shook her head, amazed at herself.

She opened her closet door and stared at its contents. Should she change out of her gown? she wondered. Or maybe greet Marc at the door in a long robe? Or in nothing at all? The thought made her giggle, which set up a giddiness that was sheer nerves and she knew it. Watch it, she told herself, aware that she was on the verge of hysterical laughter.

She flew down the stairs. There was some wine in the fridge from a dinner party she'd given a while ago. Perhaps she should have a glass, to calm her down. But she stopped halfway to the kitchen. She'd had one earlier and should probably wait for Marc to come before having another.

Oh, God. What should she do…think…be now? She stood in the kitchen doorway hugging herself, as though her arms could keep her from bursting apart.

The clock on the wall told her that it was nearly midnight and he was on his way.

Would she be relaxed and casual when he came to the door? Yes. A sophisticated woman of the world. She'd offer a calm hello, pour him a drink. They would sit together on the couch, chatting easily, until one thing led to another. A pleasant picture, Hallie thought.

Or…Marc would throw open the door, sweep her up into his arms and carry her upstairs to her bed. He wouldn't even be out of breath, he was so strong. Then he would make expert, soul-destroying, passionate love to her, twice, three times, even, until they were sated, spent, until neither of them could move a muscle.

The ringing of the doorbell startled her out of her reverie. She glanced down at herself. Still in her pink gown, her feet bare. Ah well, she thought, hurrying to the door. The decision of what she would wear had been made for her.

She opened the door to a man who was not relaxed and sophisticated. His tie and jacket were gone. Sexual intensity radiated from every pore, and Hallie stepped back at the onslaught. She was reminded of a moment in childhood when she'd stood on the safe side of a fence, watching as a bull was let in to the enclosure. The animal was enormous, every part of him, and he literally pawed the ground, bellowing, waiting for a cow to be brought to him for mounting. She remembered the moment as being both scary and exciting at the same time.

Before Hallie had a chance to say hello, Marc entered the room and closed the door behind him. He grabbed her, almost roughly, pulled her to him, and gave her a heart-stopping kiss. His tongue plundered her mouth, his hands moved restlessly over her back. He pressed her to him, closer and closer and closer, until she couldn't breathe.

It seemed fantasy number two was in operation…and she wasn't sure she wanted it to be.

When Hallie broke the kiss and pushed him away, Marc experienced a moment of disconnect. It was as though he'd been running mindlessly down a hill, gathering speed all the way, when a boulder suddenly appeared, blocking the path. Putting on the brakes took a huge effort.

"What?" he said.

But Hallie scrambled over to the couch then curled her legs up under her. Folding her arms, she ran her hands up and down them as though she were chilly. How could that be? He felt blazing hot, himself.

He remained standing at the door, his body throbbing with need, and feeling like a jerk. What had just happened?

"What?" he said again, thoroughly confused.

He saw the shiver that ran all through her. "Oh, lord," she said breathlessly, "I'm sorry. It's just that, well, I'm just a bit terrified."

"Why?"

"It's too soon."

He wiped a hand around his mouth. Too soon? Back there in the gazebo, he'd practically had her straddling him, both of them ready as all get-out. He'd arrived ready to pick up where they'd left off.

Looked like his timing was a little askew.

"Too soon?" he echoed, still trying to get his brain back into function mode.

She nodded, her eyes large and apologetic, and achingly sincere. "I mean, I want to."

"I sense a 'but' in there someplace."

She patted the seat next to her on the couch, inviting him to sit. "Can we talk first?"

He groaned silently. Talk. Women always wanted to talk. Why? he'd wondered all his adult life. Why didn't they go with what felt good, hash it out later if necessary?

Slowly, he walked over to the couch and sat so he could face her. He took her hand in his and with a half smile, said, "Sure I can't convince you to talk a little later?"

She tried to smile back, but it was obvious that she was going through something pretty serious. She looked at her lap, as though afraid to meet his gaze. Concerned now, he let go of her hand and lifted her chin with his finger, forcing her to make eye contact. In the dimly lit room, her face was porcelain, her eyes dark with apprehension.

Concern for her took over now, and his hormone-fueled tension began to ebb. "Tell me," he said gently, taking her hand again.

She played with his fingers, finding whatever she had to say difficult. Finally, she said, "I know it's the thing to do, to go to bed first and talk later, but I'm just, well, kind of old-fashioned that way. It has to mean something."

The last sentence took him by surprise and he felt

a stab of hurt at her words. He cautioned himself not to react, to go slowly here, to hear her out. "You're saying you don't engage in meaningless sex."

"Right."

"Is that what you think we, us together, would be? Meaningless?"

As much as he'd tried to mask it, she must have sensed her words had wounded him, because her eyes widened and her hand flew to her mouth. "Oh, no, Marc, far from it!"

"Well, good then," he said, relieved. "Because making love with you would mean a hell of a lot to me."

"Oh, Marc," she said. "I didn't mean to insult you. It's just that—" she sighed, made a rueful face "—well, the last time I..." She shook her head. "No, never mind."

"Tell me. The last time, what?"

"The last time I was with someone, he broke my heart."

Marc frowned. For some reason he had never thought about Hallie's past love life and the introduction of the topic wasn't something he was eager to pursue.

"When was that?"

"A year ago."

A strong surge of jealousy hit him with as much surprise as the hurt had just moments ago. "Do you still care about him?"

"Oh, no."

"Good." He took her hand again, kissed the palm, then her wrist. God, how could skin taste like honey?

She liked what he was doing, he could tell, by the way her lids lowered to half-mast and she got a look of sensuality on her face. "It's just that I promised myself I would be careful the next time." Her words came out sounding breathy.

"I can understand that." He moved his mouth up her arm to the soft spot in the crook of her elbow.

"I mean," she went on huskily, "I don't think I can take my heart being broken again."

He raised his head, gazed at her. "Hallie, what are you asking for?"

Her eyes opened slowly and reluctantly. "I'm not sure. I don't want to be treated badly or taken lightly."

Again, her words hurt, but this time he retaliated. "I'm a little confused here. You're talking like I'm some kind of womanizer, a love-'em-and-leave-'em type. What have I ever done to make you think I'd either treat you badly or take you lightly? Because if that's what you—"

"No, no," she interrupted. "I know you won't. You're an honorable man."

"Well—" he shrugged "—that's a bit of an exaggeration. But, yeah, I take my responsibilities seriously, try not to promise something I can't follow through on."

"Yes, I think I know that. It's just that, I'm a little fragile, I guess. Do you want some wine? Or coffee or something?" She started to rise, but Marc pulled her back down to the couch.

"I don't need anything. Tell me why you're fragile."

She ran a finger over the arm of the couch. "Fred turned out to be a weasel, and I didn't know it until the end, when he told me he was leaving. We were engaged, you see, due to get married in a month."

"I see."

She nodded, gazed at him. "We had picked out a house and everything. Then he got cold feet and took off. He wrote me a note, can you believe that? He didn't even end it in person."

"Obviously, the guy is a loser," Marc said sympathetically. "But better before than after."

"I know. It was just…well, I thought we wanted the same things, you see. He said he did."

"What kind of things?"

"A home, kids, roots."

"Sounds reasonable."

"And to stay, here, in Promise. At the last moment, he said he couldn't go through with it. That he had a terror of settling down."

This time there was a pause before Marc said slowly, "I see."

"So, well—" Hallie sighed, then shrugged "—that's why I got a little freaked out. I was thinking about Fred."

A silence fell, broken only by the ticking of a clock. Marc digested what he'd just found out about the woman he'd wanted, more than words could express, to share a bed with that night. And, man, did he feel let down, more than he could have ever imagined.

A deep sadness invaded him, like the lonely sound

of an owl in the night. He felt robbed, as though something precious had been put in his hand, then pulled away.

He felt her eyes on him as he stared off into space. She'd wanted to talk, and they'd talked. He was profoundly sorry they had.

"So, what you're saying," he began, "is that you aren't willing to see what happens," he said dispassionately. "If you give yourself to a man, you want to know if your basic life goals are the same, so you won't get involved with someone you have no future with."

Hallie thought it over, then said slowly, "When you put it that way, it sounds so…calculating. But yes, I guess so. It's like religion—if it's real important to you to marry in your religion, then you probably shouldn't go out with people of different faiths. Why risk it? Or if you want kids, don't go out with people who don't want kids. That kind of thing."

"Self-protection, before the fact."

"Yes. I feel things so very deeply, Marc. Too deeply, maybe. There's been so much loss in my life—my parents, Gram and Gramps, Fred. I guess, yes, I need to protect myself from more loss."

"I see."

Again, there was silence. The rain started up again, and Marc detected the faint pitter-patter of raindrops on the windows.

"I'm sorry," Hallie said. "I've kind of ruined the mood, huh."

"You might say that."

Too restless to remain seated, he stood up and

walked over to the fireplace, where he could hear raindrops echoing loudly in the chimney. He made himself take in a deep breath, then let it out again. They were having such a *civilized* conversation, he thought. When he'd come here tonight, he'd felt anything but civilized. Primal, more like it. Too bad it couldn't have stayed that way. No, they'd had to *talk* first. Damn. And the thing of it was, despite the talk and the mood change, he still wanted the woman more than ever.

Marc's temper was up, Hallie could sense it. He was frustrated, too, of course. But the anger was there, nipping at the edges of his conversation. She felt vaguely guilty for making him mad, but not for saying what she had.

After all, the stakes, for her, were high, and if she hadn't expressed what she'd been feeling, she'd have no one else to blame if there were misunderstandings later. Couldn't he see that?

She watched as he gazed up at the painting over the mantel, a decent if uninspired still life of fruit on a plate with a pitcher behind it. ''Great-great Uncle Rupert,'' she offered to his back. ''He took up painting in his eighties.''

Marc nodded at her answer to his unasked question, then turned around and leaned both elbows on the mantel. His expression was hard, and she saw the muscles in his jaw working before he spoke. ''If I were to be one hundred percent honest with you, I'd say that you're right, we probably shouldn't take this any further.''

It took a moment for his words to sink in. ''Why?''

"I thought you knew. I'm not staying here, in Promise. This is a temporary job, until Chief McKinney comes back or decides to retire. I'm only here for a few months."

"I...didn't know."

"So it seems. I thought you did."

Oh, no, she thought as disappointment filled her like water seeping into parched earth. She shook her head, unable to speak.

He went on, the granite-hard planes of his face devoid of all the compassion, humor, gentleness she knew he was capable of. "I guess I'm like Fred. I don't plan on settling down anywhere, not for a long time, if ever. You want kids, I'm not sure if I do. I think I'd make a lousy father. All I knew was discipline and punishment for not following the rules.

"But that's not the main thing. You see, Hallie, I just got out of the armed forces, where every hour of every day was planned for me, where I had no say in where I was stationed or where I got to live, or even what time I got up in the morning. Don't get me wrong, I stayed in because it was a way of life I wanted—I was used to it, I guess—and where I felt I was serving my country."

He paused, looked down as though contemplating what to say next. Then he went on, and she could sense his anger just beneath the surface. "But I'm out now, Hallie. I don't want strings, or 'have-to's of any sort. You have a great town here, and great people, and I'll be sorry to leave, but I will leave. I'll be here for a few months, tops, then I'm gone. There's too much of the world to see." He lifted his hands, then dropped them to his side. "So, there you have it," he finished with all the brutality of a sledgehammer.

"My worst nightmare."

"Sure sounds like it," he agreed.

Unbidden, tears ran down her cheeks. She wished she could stop them, but was powerless to do so. Just as she was powerless to make Marc into the man she'd wanted—and wished—him to be. "I didn't know," she said again.

"Dammit, don't cry," he said, moving away from the mantel. "Hallie, please. I didn't intend to make you unhappy."

"I know it," she said, sniffling, trying to stop the tears. "It's not you, it's me. Why don't men want to stay with me?"

He crossed back to the couch and kneeled in front of her. Taking her hands, he said, "It's got nothing to do with *you,* dammit. I *do* want to stay with you. Just not forever. Is that so difficult to understand?"

She sniffled some more, unable to speak.

He squeezed her hands, hard, as though trying to make her see the obvious. "There are all kinds of relationships, Hallie. Some are long-term, some are short, but worth it. I want you and you want me. I think we both know that nothing about how we feel is casual. We're good together, dammit."

He moved off his knees and onto the couch again. Grabbing her arm, he said, "What would you have done if when I'd walked in the door, I'd grabbed you and carried you off to bed?"

"I would have gone along with it."

"And if I'd made love to you?"

"I'd have gone along with it."

"Just gone along?" he said with a raised eyebrow.

"No. You know what I mean." She sniffled again. "And then, after we'd made love, if you told me then that you were leaving? It would have been twice as bad, because then I would know what I couldn't have anymore."

He let go of her arm and raked his short hair with his fingers. Shaking his head, he said, "It's a no-win situation, isn't it?"

"I won't have my heart broken again, Marc." She swiped at her tears with the heel of her hand. "And if we have an affair and you go, it will be. I'm not sure I have enough spirit to recover again." She looked down at her lap and continued, "I'm still holding out the hope that there will be a man, in the next few years, anyway, who loves my town and wants to build a life with me here. I really want that home, Marc. I really want those babies."

She put one hand over her heart, so filled with emotion now, that it was hard to get the words out. "I have so much love to give. I'm tired of spoiling my friends' kids, tired of being Auntie Hallie."

"Aren't you a little young to be sounding so spinsterish? You're not even thirty."

"Meg's son is six, and Joannie just told me tonight she and Tom are planning on another. I want that, Marc, I want what they have. And I want it all. I want that baby to have a mother *and* a father."

Her words disturbed him, she could tell, because he rose again, and she watched him move around her living room like a caged animal. She was struck once more with how much she truly, deeply *desired* him. Oh, how she wanted to see what it felt like to have all that energy buried deep inside her, filling her.

The sudden moisture between her legs made her blush. Here she was, telling Marc why they couldn't be together, and here was her body, betraying her.

He continued pacing, shaking his head. "You have so many plans, Hallie, don't you? So many fantasies of how you want it to be. Beware of depending on them to make you happy."

He stopped suddenly right in front of her, looked down at her, his fists clenched by his sides. "I've seen so much," he said, his voice deep, his pale eyes filled with pain. "Men blown up by land mines, jeep and helicopter accidents. Wife beatings, child abuse, suicide. It's rough out there in the big bad world. Life is cruel. At best, it's unpredictable. You of all people should know that—hell, you lost your parents at way too young an age. I believe in seeking comfort wherever we can find it. So, yeah, I hear what you're saying, but I sure don't agree with it."

Unexpectedly, she was filled with a compassion for him that bordered on grief. She wanted to touch him, but refrained from doing so. "You *have* seen a lot, haven't you? So much sadness, so much misery."

He shrugged, his face a mask. "My share. But don't start feeling sorry for me. I can take it."

"You were raised to take it."

"You got it."

He unclenched his fists and rubbed his hands together, as though to make the blood circulate again. "Look, I'd better get out of here before we start discussing philosophy and debating the existence of God.''

''Do you believe in God?''

He raised and lowered a shoulder. ''Not from what I've seen, no. But I'm open, I guess.'' Abruptly, he turned and headed for the door. She rose and followed him. With his hand on the knob he turned. The small, rueful smile on his face took her by surprise.

''So, is this where one of us says, 'I hope we can be friends'?''

''Do you think we can?'' she asked.

''I honestly don't know. I've never been friends with a woman before.''

''Why?''

''The sex thing gets in the way. And, trust me, with you, the sex thing is in the way.'' He gazed at her, stroked her cheek, once, with the back of his fingers, then dropped his hand. ''You look tired again. Get some sleep.''

''You're not angry anymore?''

''At what?''

''That it didn't happen tonight, what we both thought was going to happen?''

''Not anymore, no,'' he said ruefully. ''Disappointed as hell, yes.'' He dropped a quick kiss on her mouth, then opened the door. ''Go to bed. Without me,'' he added quickly, then was gone.

Hallie shut and double locked the door, then leaned back against it and closed her eyes. She felt as though she'd been through the wringer, and had come out the other side depleted.

And alone. Most definitely alone.

Chapter Seven

Sunday was not a good day. Marc woke up cranky and frustrated, and—although he didn't want to admit it—a feeling very much like loss lurked just beneath the surface. He wasn't one to analyze himself and his emotions too deeply; all he knew was that he wanted the pain to go away. So, he did what he'd always done in the past: he got busy.

He finished unpacking some boxes, then cleaned up around his small rented cottage on the edge of town. He broke down the boxes and hauled them into the garage. Then he got into his sweats and running shoes and took off, up and down several steep streets in town, then along back roads. After a couple of hours of this, he'd worked up a good sweat, but didn't feel any better.

Irritated with himself, he fixed himself a big meal of bacon and eggs and toast, read the local paper, then the *San Francisco Chronicle*. He noted that there were still small wars being waged in all parts of the world, but he no longer had to wonder if he would be shipped out, sent overseas, put in the line of fire.

Those days had been over for several years anyway, since he'd been chosen for the elite investigation unit and had been sent to Quantico for intensive FBI training. This had qualified him for the life he'd intended to lead, post-military, in law enforcement.

There was still the entire afternoon to kill, so he did some laundry at the Laundromat in town, then got onto his Harley and tooled along Highway One, taking the curves too quickly, feeling the wind in his face, glorying in the sense of danger but knowing he was in control.

He flew past impressive scenery, most especially admiring the groves of Monterey pines, those tall, ancient trees that had spent hundreds of years being swept sideways by the wind and, instead of being destroyed by the wind's force, had just bent their branches and continued to survive whatever onslaught came their way.

He'd thought he was like those trees—strong, adaptable and, no matter what, still functioning. Yeah, well, he thought bitterly, a survivor he might be, but today, there was something keeping him from rejoicing in that fact.

Hallie.

He played back the evening with her. Could he have done it better, made it turn out differently? If he were another kind of man, he might have told her he didn't know what his plans were, and that he was open to settling down.

But he knew that wasn't so. When Len had called him up with this offer, it had been exactly what he was looking for: temporary civilian life in the work area he wanted to pursue, ''temporary'' being the operative word. Something that would look good on a future resumé in the unlikely event he changed his mind and decided to land in one place and stay there.

He would *not* tie himself down to anything or anyone, he told himself fiercely, especially not to a particular town. Of that he was certain. But that certainty gave him no joy, not when something important— something he'd not been aware he was missing—was now in view, and he couldn't have it.

That something was Hallie. He wanted her. Sure, it was about sex; it had been a while since his last brief affair with a woman who was just as willing as he was to have no strings, no promises of forever. But he knew it was more than his body's need he was dealing with here.

Dammit, why couldn't he have her? Why couldn't he have her sweetness and honesty and just plain goodness in his life?

Why did there always have to be complications when it came to women and dealing with them? She'd come to mean more to him than he wanted any woman to mean.

Not for the first time, Marc was baffled by this attraction toward her. She was a funny combination of a modern independent woman, mixed with a healthy dose of old-fashioned homey, helpful, small-town attitude. Hallie was a nester type, a putter-down of roots, and he'd never been drawn to wholesomeness, never.

Whatever she was, he craved her, this sunny woman with the strawberry-blond hair, the first woman who had ever gotten beneath his skin.

And that knowledge downright terrified him.

By evening, when he should have been admiring the setting sun, with all the gold and pink colors of the spectrum represented, he was still irritated, bordering on angry. With Hallie mostly, but with himself, too. He wanted to pound his fist into something and relieve the tension. He'd done some amateur boxing in the service; maybe he would find a gym tomorrow, work off some of this anger.

Because if he didn't, it might build into a volcano of unstoppable rage, and he never wanted to go there.

Never.

Hallie was so exhausted, she thought of calling in sick Monday morning, but she didn't want to leave Meg without someone to cover her station. Instead, she dragged herself off to work. Once there, she tended to her tables, all the while keeping an eye out for Marc, who never showed up. With a start, she realized that, in one short week, she'd begun to look for him each day. Before she'd met him, she'd always enjoyed her work at Java. Now a sense of disappointment dogged her hours here.

During a lull in the breakfast service, Meg came up to her near the counter with a broad smile on her face. "So, how're we feeling today?"

"Okay," Hallie replied with an answering smile that took all the effort she could muster.

"You look pretty tired, kid. Someone been keeping you busy?" she asked, one eyebrow raised knowingly.

"No, I just didn't sleep too well."

"Well, I sure hope you didn't," she said cheerfully. "I want details."

"Meg, really, I—"

"Hallie," Robbie called out, "here's your double stack, side of bacon for table eight."

"Thanks." She picked up the order and hustled off with it, grateful to be away from Meg's curiosity.

"On your break," Meg called after her. "I'm available for girl talk."

Girl talk? Ha! Hallie thought. She had nothing to share because nothing had happened. She knew Meg and Joannie, her two dearest friends, had all kinds of expectations about the new man in her life. They would be almost as disappointed as she was that there was nothing to report.

All day yesterday she'd worked on putting Marc out of her mind. Morning till nighttime, she'd tried to turn off the attraction she felt toward him, telling herself she had to do so, before her feelings took on a life of their own. But it was like the old saying went: she was trying to close the barn door after the horse had already escaped.

She cared, deeply, about the tall policeman. Without being consciously aware of it, all week she'd been indulging in large-scale fantasies about him and the life they might lead together.

She knew that it was way too soon for such thoughts. He'd only been here a week! And they'd only kissed—well, kissed and a bit more. They hadn't really gone out on a date, for heaven's sake, and had spoken only briefly about likes and dislikes, food preferences, music—all the small details a woman needed to know about a person before she allowed her heart to become involved.

But it was too late, she was honest enough to admit to herself. She missed him this morning. Missed his smile, his gentle kidding. Missed taking an order for the enormous amount of food he ate with gusto, without showing any of it on his well-developed body, which had not an ounce of fat on it.

Turn it off, she told herself again. *Pull back.*

But it was impossible to pull back from caring about Marc. She already recognized in herself all the signs of falling in love.

She'd been jealous when he danced with others on Saturday night, even when he always came back to her. She'd pooh-poohed all her friends when they'd kidded her about the two of them, but had felt a secret pride that this man, this *hunk,* found her desirable, wanted to dance with her, wanted to be with her.

She'd been scared and excited when he was on his way back to her place afterwards, ready to go to bed with him because it had felt so right. She wouldn't have all these feelings unless her heart was deeply engaged.

So why had she put the brakes on? Because, after Fred's abrupt departure, she'd promised herself that, if a new man caught her interest, she would tell him about her priorities before becoming involved. She knew it was the mature, responsible, grown-up thing to do.

But, she had to admit, part of her was sorry she'd even brought it up, because she felt cheated out of an experience she'd hungered for so much she'd fairly danced out of her skin. He would be a wonderful lover, she just knew it. He moved like a man confident of his masculinity. And experienced—there was no way a man who looked and carried himself like Marc did wouldn't have had a lot of lovers.

Had he ever been in love? She hadn't asked him. Had his heart been broken? Again, she hadn't asked him. The discussion had been all about her. Maybe she should have explored his history more, got him to talk about himself and his past. Maybe that would have given her a clue to his state of mind, helped her to understand him a little better.

Offered some hope for the two of them.

But no, that was what women always did. Thought that if they understood the man better, they could find a way to make him change. People didn't change, not really. You needed to accept them as they were, and if the way they were wasn't acceptable, you needed to stop it before it started.

Which was what had happened.

But still…

Oh, Marc, Hallie thought as her shift ended and she transferred her tips to her purse, *it could have been so good, for both of us.* Instead, she was left with regret that he'd come into her life in the first place.

On her way out to her car, she heard Meg calling to her. "Hallie, wait up."

She didn't really want to talk to Meg, not now, not when her feelings were so raw. Still, she waited at her car door, as her boss and friend came up to her. She owed her. This was the woman who had offered her a job last year, knowing she had no previous experience waiting on tables but aware she needed a full-time job now that Gram was gone, and who had been willing to take a chance on her.

"Hey," the tall redhead said, standing in front of her, hands on her hips and concern in her eyes. "What's wrong?"

She made a rueful face. "I don't really want to talk about it."

"Is this about you and Marc?"

"Please, Meg, not now."

Meg's face turned serious. "What happened? Did he hurt you? Some of those military guys can get kind of rough."

She put a hand on her friend's arm. "No, nothing like that, I promise."

"Well, okay then," Meg said, doubt still lingering in her light green eyes. "Because if he did anything to you—" She left the sentence unfinished, looking fierce as an ancient Amazon warrior.

"Thanks. You're a dear."

"So, what then? You two looked so good on the dance floor, and it was obvious, when you left, that your evening wasn't over yet."

When Hallie didn't reply, Meg said, "I'm sorry, I'm prying. It's just that I worry about you, and you looked so happy with him.'' She shrugged, embarrassed. ''Joannie and I, well, we thought you'd never let anyone near you again after Fred took a hike. And it was so nice, you know, to see that all hope is not lost.''

Hallie wondered how much to tell her, how much there actually was to tell. She considered, then after a few moments, said, ''We want different things, that's all. He wants an affair, and I'm looking for something more long-term.''

Meg's brows furrowed. ''Well, yeah, but that's how long-term things start, with an affair, right? I mean, anyone who's not blind could see the two of you have the hots for each other, pardon my crudity. Most of the couples I know start out that way, and then, if it's meant to last longer, it develops.''

''I know.'' Hallie sighed. ''But he's pretty adamant. He'll be leaving in a few months, and I'll be staying and, well, I didn't think I could get through another one of those. He's too much like Fred.''

''Are you kidding?'' Meg snorted. ''He's nothing like Fred. Frankly, and I've never told you this, I'm glad it didn't work out for you two. Fred was a jerk. You can do better. Marc is better.''

''Did you really think Fred was a jerk? Why didn't you ever tell me?''

Meg shrugged. ''I assumed you saw something in him I didn't. Besides, we're all attracted to different things in people. Who am I to say who's right for someone? My track record isn't the best, to put it mildly.''

Meg was a widow who'd come to Promise a few

years earlier with nothing but her toddler son and a dream of opening a restaurant. In the time Hallie had known her, she'd had a few men in her life, but nothing long-lasting.

"Yeah," Meg went on, "I figured maybe Fred was the type that was a hidden treasure, and you'd found the key. But now that he's history, I say, good for you. Hold out for the prize."

"Marc isn't the prize," she said with a sad smile. "But thanks for telling me what you thought about Fred. It helps me to feel less like a loser myself."

"A loser? You? Are you kidding? If anyone deserves love, it's you." She took Hallie's hand and squeezed it. "You'll find it. If not this one, then another will come along. You wait and see."

Hallie wanted to cry at her friend's loyalty. Instead, she hugged her and said, "You're the best," got into her car and went home.

As she stepped out of the shower half an hour later, she heard the phone in her bedroom ringing. Wrapping herself in a towel, she rushed in to answer it.

"Hallie?"

It was Marc. Her heart soared quickly at the sound of his voice.

"Yes?"

"I thought you'd want to know. We sent all the fingerprints we found on the candlesticks to the lab, and we got a hit on one pair."

"Oh."

He hadn't called to talk to her about the two of them; he'd called about the robbery. She tried to push down the feeling of disappointment. This was good news, she told herself. This was progress, wasn't it? Two days had passed and she hadn't heard again from Tracy, nor had the stolen objects shown up. So, she ought to be grateful that there was a break in the case.

"Well, good," she told him.

"Ordinarily I wouldn't report this to you until we'd checked it out, but, well, I thought you deserved to know."

"Thank you, Marc."

"We're going to follow up on it today. The prints are from an ex-con who lives in San Francisco, named Gus Madison. You know anyone by that name?"

"No."

"Not familiar at all?"

"Never heard of him."

"All right then. I've called the San Francisco PD and asked them to send an officer over there, but they're stretched kind of thin today—some kind of parade. So, I'm going to run over there myself, check it out. Don't get your hopes up. It could mean nothing. He could have visited the museum, handled the candlesticks. Could have picked them up at the shop in Santa Cruz. But, it's worth a try."

"I appreciate it. Should I come along?"

"Don't even think about it," Marc said in a tone that brooked no argument. "Ex-cons can be pretty unsavory, and this one did time for armed robbery. I won't put you in danger."

"I see. Well, thanks for calling. You'll let me know?"

"As soon as I know anything."

"Thanks."

She waited a moment longer, and could have sworn he was about to say something. Instead, without another word, he hung up.

He'd mentioned nothing about what had transpired between them on Saturday night. Not that she would have expected it; he was doing his job.

Actually, he was doing more than his job. Making a follow-up visit himself, instead of waiting a day for the local police, or instead of sending one of his men to check on this Gus person.

Hallie didn't know much about law enforcement, but she was pretty sure the chief of police didn't go out on this kind of routine check. She was being given special treatment, and that made the area around her heart warm up a bit.

Suddenly, it hit her. There was a good chance that the man who had ''helped'' Tracy with the robbery was this ex-con. This man with a history of using a gun. Tracy had always liked to live on the wild side— had she hooked up with someone really dangerous this time?

Oh, God, she thought wildly, what if Tracy was in this ex-con's apartment, with him, right this moment? Was she in some kind of danger?

That did it. Hallie had to get to Tracy before Marc did, or at least be there if she was, indeed, at Gus's apartment. Her immature, brainless cousin was in over her head, for sure.

Without bothering to think it through, she quickly pulled on a pair of jeans and a sweatshirt. She would hurry down to police headquarters, only a few blocks away, and follow Marc into the city. She'd never tailed anyone before, and it probably wasn't a real brilliant idea to do so now, especially when the person she was following was an experienced law officer. But she would do it anyway.

Whatever happened, she would be there when— and if—Tracy needed her. And then she'd kill her cousin for putting her through all of this.

Marc hadn't been to San Francisco in years, and back then, he'd taken public transportation, so he'd never driven the narrow hills of that city. Maneuvering his SUV around moving vans, buses and cyclists, not to mention avoiding pedestrians who didn't obey traffic lights, took every bit of his concentration. He finally found the area they called the Castro District and headed up a street that would be considered an alleyway in any other city, until he spotted the address he'd gotten from Madison's parole officer.

Since there was no parking available, he drove up and down several impossibly constricted streets, searching for a parking spot. He finally found one four blocks away, squeezed his vehicle into a space meant for one several inches shorter, and got out.

He walked quickly back to the address he'd been given. It was a four-story brownstone that had seen better days. An adjacent empty lot was filled with weeds and litter, there was an overturned garbage can on the sidewalk in front of the building, and two disheveled-looking men sat on the stoop drinking from bottles wrapped in brown paper sacks.

Ignoring the men, Marc ran up the stairs, noted that the "security" door was missing a lock, pushed it open, and went in.

Hallie was just about out of breath as she came around a corner to see Marc heading up the stairs to an apartment building. From what she could tell, he had no idea he'd been followed, for which she was extremely grateful.

She'd done as she'd seen in all the movies, kept three or four cars behind him, never coming close. It had been almost impossible to follow him when they'd entered the city, and she'd actually run two red lights. Thank heavens, no one had stopped her for doing so. When he'd parked, the only place close enough had been in front of a fire hydrant, so she'd taken it. If she lost him now, she knew, she'd never find him again.

She'd broken so many laws today, she was sure something terrible was going to happen to her. She didn't even jaywalk, for heaven's sake, and she took none of this casually. Only for Tracy, she thought grimly, would she do this.

One of the men on the outside steps made an extremely lewd comment to her as Hallie stumbled up the stairs. Her face flushed at his suggestion of what she might do for him.

Once inside the door with the broken lock, she scanned the mailboxes, but there was no Madison on them. There were two apartment doors on the first floor and no Marc in sight, so slowly, carefully, she began to climb the stairs. She was terrified as to what he'd do if he found her there, but overriding her fear was concern for her troubled cousin.

Up ahead, she heard the sound of footsteps running quickly up the stairs, so she followed the sound until she was near the top of the last staircase. The hallways smelled foul, a mixture of garbage, urine and vomit, and she held her hand over her nose so the smell wouldn't make her retch. On the third to last step, she stopped and crouched over, not at all eager for Marc to see her. Quaking with dread, she listened intently.

She heard the sound of knocking on the door, followed by Marc calling out, "Gus Madison, open up!"

There was no answer.

Now Marc pounded harder on the door. "Police! Open up!" he called again, but again, there was silence. Crouching even more till her body was bent practically double, Hallie climbed to the top step and peeked over the banister.

Marc had his back to her at the door, and he was jiggling the doorknob.

From within, there came a faint sound. A dog? No, it was a high-pitched wailing noise, like someone in pain.

Her heart beating with exertion and terror, Hallie watched as Marc took out his gun and flicked off the safety latch. Holding the gun in his right hand, pointed upward, he backed up to the landing, then surged forward, his broad shoulder to the door. It splintered under the impact and he disappeared inside.

All fear of being caught vanished as Hallie bounded up the last step and followed him in. There, in a small, messy room, was an unmade bed and dresser. On the bed was Tracy, her hands tied behind her back, the rope looped across the headboard, and a red handkerchief over her mouth!

Marc, still unaware of Hallie's presence in the doorway, held his gun at the ready as he opened first a closet door, then the door to the bathroom. Satisfied there was no one else in the room, he hurried over to the bed and removed the handkerchief from Tracy's mouth.

The first word she uttered was "Hallie!"

Marc spun around, his face registering surprise, at first, then quickly turning to a fierce anger.

Lowering his gun, he bellowed, "What the hell are you doing here?"

Chapter Eight

Without answering his question, Hallie swept past him and ran to the young woman on the bed. Quickly, she untied the ropes that bound her hands behind her, then pulled her arms free and hugged her tightly.

"Oh, Hallie," the young woman cried and allowed herself to be hugged. "I'm such a fool."

"Are you all right?" she asked her. "Did he hurt you?"

"No, no, I'm fine."

Recovering swiftly from the shock of seeing Hallie behind him, Marc holstered his gun as he watched the two women rock back and forth together, both of them sobbing their hearts out. He gave them a brief moment to indulge their emotions, then decided to take charge.

"Hallie," he said sternly. When she continued to hug the young woman on the bed, he said, more forcefully now, "Hallie! Tell me what's going on."

She glanced over at him, her tear-streaked face registering both relief and guilt. "This is my cousin, Tracy Fitzgerald."

As the situation didn't call for any kind of polite response on his part, he glowered at the slender, dark-blond young woman. "Ms. Fitzgerald, where is Madison?"

"G-g-gone," Tracy said, sniffling through her tears.

"Was he the one who did this to you, tied you up and gagged you?"

She nodded, looking like a bewildered waif on a poster trying to recruit aid for needy children.

"Do you know where he went?"

"N-n-no."

"How long's he been gone?"

"I'm not sure. An hour or so."

"Does he have the stolen goods?"

"I guess so. But it's all my fault!" she wailed and burst into tears again.

"Hush, now," Hallie said. "Don't say anything else."

That one threw Marc for a loop. "Why shouldn't she? Don't you want to get your things back?"

"Tracy," Hallie said, standing up, but keeping her hand on her cousin's shoulder. "I'd like you to meet our new chief of police, Marc Walcott."

She said this pointedly, as though warning her cousin that they were in the presence of the enemy. But, dammit, he wasn't the enemy, he was the good guy.

"The chief of police?" Tracy repeated, her eyes wide with awe.

"That's right," he said. "And I want to know what the hell is going on here. Care to explain?"

It didn't seem as though she did, for, again, she just gazed at him wordlessly. Marc shot an accusing look at Hallie, then directed more questions to her cousin.

"Did he kidnap you, or did the two of you set it up?" In other words, was Hallie's cousin a victim or an accomplice?

"Don't say a word, Tracy," Hallie warned, her hand tightening on her cousin's shoulder.

He stomped toward her, really irritated now. "What is your problem, Hallie? Why are you telling her that? She's the only one who knows what's gone down, the only chance you have of getting back the things that were stolen. Haven't you been telling me how much they mean to you?"

Hallie swallowed, glanced at her cousin, then looked back at him, her chin jutted out defiantly. "Maybe they weren't stolen. Maybe they were—" again, she swallowed "—borrowed. Right, Tracy?"

"Huh?" her cousin said.

"You're protecting her," Marc said.

"And you're badgering her."

Man, was he getting heated. Rising to his full height, he inhaled and shot her The Look. This time, by God, she would cower under it.

"I'm trying to get to the bottom of what's going on," he said through gritted teeth. He could feel his temper going up, up, up. He slammed his fist on the small dresser near the bed. "Dammit, I'm trying to help you."

He saw her flinch at the force of his anger, could have sworn her hands were shaking. But then, she seemed to gather her courage so that she could face him without backing down, as she had done the first day they'd met.

"You can help me by letting me leave, with Tracy. It's obvious she's distressed and needs to go home with me. Right now."

With that, Hallie pulled her cousin off the bed and began to march her out of the room.

"Hold it right there!" Marc said, taking a pair of handcuffs out from a rear pocket. "I'm placing her under arrest."

Hallie turned and put her hands over her mouth in horror. "No, Marc. Please."

"She's the only lead we have," he said, walking toward her. "I have no choice."

It was clear to him now what had happened and he wanted to kick himself for not having put it together before. Tracy was the connection between Madison and the museum, the reason there had been no obvious break-in. The cousin knew the code, knew which articles were valuable, knew where to park so no one would hear anything, knew Hallie's schedule. It was a no-brainer. On the face of it, Tracy was guilty as hell.

"Marc, please," Hallie said again. "Don't arrest her. Let me take her home. She's my cousin, Marc. She's not a criminal, I promise you."

He hesitated, and in that moment he knew that he

was about to do something really stupid. By all rights he should detain the young woman, read her her rights, and take her in on charges of being an accomplice to burglary.

But, on the off-chance Tracy had been held captive, coerced or threatened—not to mention the mental image he had of Hallie's horrified face as he led her cousin off in handcuffs—he held back from doing so. It went against the grain, but there it was—one more example of how his feelings for Hallie were getting in the way of him doing his job.

Furious with himself, he said, "All right. Take her home."

"Thank you," Hallie whispered and led her cousin from the room. Down all four flights of steps the two women hurried, Marc right on their heels and shaking his head with frustration. He watched them walking purposefully down the block, Hallie with a protective arm around her cousin's shoulder, not looking back.

"I'll be by later to talk to her, so make sure you don't go anywhere!" he called after them, then stopped, propped his hands on his hips. "Hallie?" he called again. "Do I have your promise? I've bent the rules for you, and now I'd like your word. Do I have it?"

He held his breath, waiting to see what she'd do next. Given her innate sense of fair play, he was pretty sure he knew what her answer would be, but relief surged through him when she slowed her pace, then stopped. After she conferred with Tracy, she turned around. "You have my word," she called out. "We'll be at the house."

The two women moved on, disappearing around the corner.

Shaking his head, he watched them go, muttering a low curse at himself for his actions.

Today, he'd been singularly ineffective in arousing fear or even getting any respect—from Hallie, at least. He had compromised his principles. Hell, he'd even been tailed by a rank amateur and hadn't sensed a thing. Talk about being off his game.

It was because he was distracted, he knew that. By Hallie, his feelings for her, their relationship, or non-relationship, to put it in perspective. Never in his life had he let a woman interfere with his work, his goals, his performance on the job.

Straighten up, soldier.

His father's voice rang in his head, as it always did when Marc was on the verge of feeling sorry for himself. It was done, over, history, the old man would tell him. *Move on.* And, most of all, *Clean up your own mess.*

All right then, he decided. No more berating himself. And no more falling down on the job. Action was what was called for.

He took out his cell phone. After placing a call to his office, he asked for Captain Coe and barked out orders to find out the license number and make of whatever vehicle was owned by an ex-con named Gus Madison, then put out an APB on it. If he didn't own a car, then Coe was to run a check on all recent rentals, known friends, the whole nine yards.

Hallie Fitzgerald and her cousin might have decided not to cooperate in this investigation, might even be putting obstacles in his path, but he had an open burglary report to investigate.

Whether the two women liked it or not, he would do his job.

As they drove back to Promise, Hallie glanced at her cousin. Not for the first time in their lives together, what she felt toward the slender young woman was exasperation mixed with concern. She'd bailed Tracy out of many scrapes in the past, but this was the most serious one yet.

"All right now, tell me what happened," she said in as no-nonsense a manner as she could, even though she was still shaking inside from the confrontation with Marc. She felt horrible. She'd been so unfair to him. When she'd hustled Tracy out of that tacky little room, she'd been quaking with dread, sure he'd change his mind and arrest both of them on the spot.

Later, she promised herself, later on she would explain it all to him, get him to understand. Now though, her priority was her cousin, and slowly, to accompanying sobs and excuses, Tracy's story came out.

When Gus had suggested they pull off a "pseudo" robbery and get Tracy's inheritance, she'd gone along. However, she soon lost any say in the matter. He was the one who suggested the ransom calls to a pay phone. He was the one who took charge, until Tracy realized she was in a lot deeper than she'd planned.

When she tried to talk Gus into returning the valuables, he'd laughed at her. He'd made some "inquiries,'' he told her, and found out that what they'd stolen would bring in a hell of a lot more than twenty-five grand. More like ten times that amount.

When she'd refused to go along with him fencing the goods, he'd tied her up and taken off, his van loaded with bounty.

"I feel awful, Hallie," her cousin said, her face wet with tears, "for putting you through all this. I swear, if you let me, I'll make it up to you. I'll never do anything like this again, I promise."

"You've said that before."

"I know, I know. I thought you were the enemy. No more, I swear. Oh, Hallie, will you ever forgive me?"

"My forgiveness is beside the point," she said tiredly. "You just about broke my heart and it will take a while to heal. I'm praying we get all the museum's belongings back, because if we don't, I don't know what I'll do."

She glanced over at her cousin, who was sobbing uncontrollably, and despite her anger at her, she felt herself softening. What good would punishing her do? She was already beating herself up enough for both of them.

"Right now, though," Hallie said, "we need to see just how much of a mess you're in. I have no experience with this kind of thing. We need to talk to a lawyer."

Tracy's hand flew to her mouth. "You mean I could be in trouble? Real trouble?"

"You got it. That's why I had you keep your mouth shut back there. Marc's the police, and anything you said to him could be used against you in a court of law, as they say on *Law and Order*. You're irresponsible and thoughtless, but you're not a crook, and I don't think you deserve to go to jail.''

Tracy looked at her, wide-eyed with fear. ''Oh, Hallie, do you think I will? Go to jail, I mean?''

''Not if I have anything to say about it.''

Marc posted himself in the hallway outside the courtroom, his arms folded across his chest, waiting. She would be here soon. And when she showed, he would let her have it, but good.

Since that stupid scene at Madison's apartment, he'd been seething with resentment against Hallie. For the past several days, poison had simmered through his bloodstream, looking for an outlet. It hadn't lessened any over that time, not even when the news came in that the Oakland PD had caught Madison with a truckload of stolen property and had hauled him in. Not even when Madison had been transferred to Promise early this morning, sneering with defiance, and Marc had been a little rough with him while removing his handcuffs.

No, his anger wasn't at Gus Madison or Tracy, but at Hallie. He'd finally put it all together, all the cumulative sins. From the first, that day at the phone booth, she'd held back information. Important information that could have cracked the case earlier, such as the ransom calls, and Hallie's own knowledge that Tracy was probably involved.

He was honest enough with himself to admit that some of his anger was caused by a feeling of betrayal.

Even if he and Hallie weren't going to have an affair, and had no future together, still, he'd felt close to her, intimate even, and he knew she'd felt the same. In his book, intimacy meant you trusted the other guy. She'd betrayed that trust.

He'd spent hours working on her case, even though someone lower on the rung should have been handling it. But because of who she was and what she'd meant to him, he'd given it his personal attention. He'd tracked down the perp, found her cousin, recovered the stolen goods before they were dispersed to the four corners of the earth.

And what had she done in return? She'd stonewalled him.

To add insult to injury—and this was the part that really got him, but good—clever lawyering meant that the bad guys weren't even going to be punished.

He felt his neck stiffen with anger, so he unfolded his arms and rotated his shoulders, trying to work out the tension. He needed to see Hallie, get this behind him.

And like that, she appeared from around the corner, walking purposefully, her heels clicking on the marble floor. Accompanying her were Tracy and an older woman who was her lawyer, a former circuit judge who had opened a part-time practice in Promise a few years ago.

Hallie wore a pale-yellow blouse, a dark-green jacket, matching skirt, and heels. She looked extremely business-like, and Marc realized that he'd seen her in many outfits on many occasions, but she always took him by surprise. Her personality seemed to take on whatever clothing she wore.

Today, in her suit, she appeared not only more formal but formidable. That sweet vulnerability of hers, which she'd allowed him to glimpse often, was nowhere in sight.

The moment Hallie saw Marc staring at her, stony-faced, outside the courtroom, she wanted to turn around and run. But she knew she wouldn't do that; she had to face him.

"I'll be right in," she told her cousin and the lawyer and watched as they pulled open the tall oak doors to the courtroom and disappeared inside.

Then she walked over to Marc, planted herself in front of him and let her gaze lock onto his. His half-lidded eyes revealed nothing.

"I owe you an apology," she began, then had to swallow down the lump that had formed in the back of her throat.

He leaned his massive body back against the marble wall and crossed his arms over his chest. "Do you?"

"Yes. Oh, Marc, I'm so sorry."

He gazed at her dispassionately for a moment longer before he raised one fierce eyebrow. "What particular transgression are you apologizing for?"

"For everything. Starting with what I did the other day. For one, I followed you to the city after you'd expressly told me not to come along."

"You did a pretty good job. I didn't spot you."

"That's because you weren't looking for me."

"That shouldn't have mattered."

Oops, Hallie thought. Marc was angry at himself for not recognizing her car. His male pride had been attacked, she supposed.

At any rate, she had more to say. "And then I took advantage of our…friendship, and didn't let you arrest Tracy. I thought it was the prudent thing to do—I still do. But I am sorry I had to do it, especially to you."

Now his gaze roamed her face slowly, as though he were checking there for discrepancies, searching for lies. He wasn't making this easy for her, but then, she didn't deserve leniency.

He pushed himself away from the wall, and she took an involuntary step backward as he did. He really was so very large.

"And what about what's going to happen in there?" He yanked his thumb at the closed courtroom door. "You sorry for that, too?"

Gone was neutral, assessing Marc. In its place was a man who was deeply upset.

"What *is* going to happen in there?"

"A deal," he muttered. "Against my recommendation, I might add. Not that that means much."

"A deal?"

"See, because the case isn't black-and-white law, there's room for interpretation. There are 'extenuating circumstances,' he added bitterly. "In essence, as your cousin is part owner of the museum, she stole from herself. Or so the lawyer is saying. She's very clever, worth whatever you're paying her, because Tracy is getting off with a slap on the wrist."

Hallie breathed out a sigh of relief and closed her eyes. "Thank God."

"See if you thank Him for this one: Madison walks, too."

Her eyes snapped open. "Oh, no," she said, her relief short-lived. "I didn't know that."

"Didn't you?"

She shook her head slowly. Then, spotting the stone bench a few feet away, she walked over and sat down on it. She was shocked and upset about this last part.

Marc might have intended to give Hallie a piece of his mind, but her sincere apology and open face had had the effect on him of a pail of water thrown on a fire. There might be some residual smoke in the air, but the main, dangerous element in the center was history.

He followed her over to the bench and stood, his hands in his pants pocket, looking down at her.

She angled her head up to meet his gaze. "I sure wouldn't mind if Gus Madison wound up behind bars."

"But not Tracy."

She had the grace to look embarrassed, then she sighed loudly. "You got me, Marc. I guess I'm guilty of a double standard. It's just that, well, he's a hardened criminal and he's the one who sold the candlesticks and took off with the goods. I mean, he really does have larceny in his heart. Tracy's just guilty of poor judgment and a refusal to grow up. It's night-and-day different."

"A crime's a crime," he said in a no-nonsense manner. "They both committed burglary."

"Yes, I know." She spread her hands in an age-old gesture that called for understanding. "What would you have me do? What if it happened to your sister or someone you loved? Wouldn't you do your best to keep her out of jail?"

He considered her words, even as he tried to hold on to the last vestiges of his anger at her. But it had evaporated. When had that happened? he asked himself. He hadn't vented, he hadn't gotten justice; the need for both had just…gone away.

Slowly, he lowered himself onto the stone bench next to her, propped his elbows on his knees, his hands clasped together between his legs. "Yeah, for someone I love, yes, I guess I would do all that I could for them. Most definitely keep them out of jail, if at all possible. It's a pretty nasty place." He shook his head. "It just ticks me off that Madison gets off so lightly as a result."

"He gets away scot-free?"

"Either they're both guilty or neither one is. Your cousin said it all started out as a joke. The D.A. was skeptical, but as Tracy's record is clean, and as she—as your lawyer put it—stole from herself, he agreed to drop the charges. The D.A. tried to get her to implicate Madison, but she refused. Wouldn't say a word against him, not even for tying her up and leaving her."

Hallie nodded. "She's feeling so guilty, she's practically wearing a hair shirt, which I guess is a good thing. Maybe she'll actually learn something from this, like how to take responsibility for her actions."

They sat, side by side, for a few moments. Then he heard her sigh, and looked over at her just as she stood up. "I have to go in," she told him. "I'm glad you've told me what to expect. After our meeting with the D.A., I had no idea what would happen in court today."

"My pleasure," he said, and she smiled at the irony in his tone.

"I thought maybe if I dropped the original complaint, that would take care of everything, but they said it was too late to do that. The whole thing is a mess. And I just want my stuff back."

He stood, adjusted his clothing. "Well, we don't need it for evidence anymore, do we? I'll have it sent over tomorrow morning."

The smile on her face made it shine. The old Hallie—his Hallie—was back. She placed a hand on his arm, lightly.

"Thanks, Marc. Do you forgive me? It would mean a lot if you did."

Shaking his head, he offered up a no-big-deal smile. "Don't think about it, Hallie. You did what you had to do, and I did what I had to do, that's all. No forgiveness necessary."

Hallie watched as Marc walked over to the courtroom door and put a hand on the knob, preparing to open it for her. Instead of following him, she stayed where she was, trying to think of what to say or do next. What she did know was that she was unable to move, unwilling to leave his presence.

She wanted more. She wanted to talk about her feelings for Marc, which were so strong at that moment, she didn't trust herself to speak. He'd taken her apology so well, better than she deserved.

Sure, she'd sensed his anger and frustration, but he hadn't punished her with it. She'd heard his disappointment with how everything had worked out. She appreciated the way he'd heard her plea for special treatment for her cousin, how he'd considered it and, finally, admitted that he might do the same for a loved one.

And through it all, she'd been impressed by his rock-hard inner strength and sense of fair play. His solid work ethic, dedication to the rules and his awareness that sometimes you had to go around them. His control of a temper that could be horribly damaging. Marc Walcott was, all in all, the most admirable man she'd ever known.

And she wanted him. Wanted his touch, the feel of him inside her. Wanted him next to her in the night and to talk to over cornflakes in the morning.

And so she stood there, outside the courtroom, and admitted to herself what she'd been unable to admit for over a week.

It was too late to worry about falling in love with Marc.

She already had.

Chapter Nine

When she heard the sound of a honking horn, Hallie grabbed the keys, raced out the kitchen door, through the hedge and onto the narrow, bush-lined driveway that bordered the museum. Marc was there; behind him was a police van. Two uniformed officers were in the process of unloading its contents.

"I've brought the—" Marc said.

But Hallie quickly ran past him, shouting, "Yes!" with exhilaration, one fist pumping in the air. At the van, she watched, her hands clasped under her chin, as her treasures were brought out.

First there was a large oil painting, then a cardboard carton filled with smaller items—a snuff box, another pair of candlesticks, pewter this time, a miniature portrait, several wood-framed needlepoints. Peering into the back of the van, she could see the old, jewel-encrusted swords brought over by early

Spanish explorers and handed down through many
generations.

Shawls, silver ornaments, a box of valuable books,
first editions many of them. A wooden statue of Jesus,
another of the Virgin Mary, both carved by early Native American converts to Catholicism. A tapestry of
a unicorn that dated from the Middle Ages. And
perched atop another box, three large dolls, all of
them dressed in hand-stitched Victorian finery.

Hallie put her clasped hands over her mouth, so
overcome with emotion it was difficult to speak.

''I'm pretty sure that's everything.''

Whirling around, she saw Marc standing behind
her, a look of grim satisfaction on his face. She nodded as, unbidden, her eyes filled with tears.

His look changed to one of concern for her. ''Don't
cry,'' he said. ''Please.''

''Can't help it,'' she said with a laugh. ''This is all
so wonderful, to have my things back. Let me get the
door.''

Quickly, she ran to the front of the museum and
unlocked the thick oak door, then turned off the
alarm. Still bursting with energy, her eyes dry now,
she stood aside as the two men brought the first load
through it. She could swear the old building bright-
ened up as, one by one, its belongings were restored.

Mark stood just outside the door, reading off from
a checklist he had in a file folder while Hallie ran
around as each item was brought in, instructing the
officers as to the general area they belonged in. Later,
after they all left, she would get Tracy to help her put
everything back in place. She would rehang the tap-

estry, polish the silver, wipe dust off the dolls. Restore order to her museum, restore order to her heritage, to the heritage of the town she adored so, the town that had taken a five-year-old orphan under its wing and nourished her into adulthood, allowing her to grow up strong and sturdy and loved.

"Where's your cousin?" Marc asked.

"Inside, resting."

"How's she doing?"

Hallie drew her attention away from the treasures for a moment. It was nice of him to ask after Tracy, especially since she knew Marc thoroughly disapproved of how her cousin had managed to escape all consequences of her actions. What he didn't know was that Hallie had plans, lots of them, to get her younger cousin into shape.

"She's doing all right," she told him. "She managed to catch a whopper of a cold, so she's in bed. Oh, that goes upstairs," she told the men who were currently balancing a carved wood tapestry fire screen that was a lot heavier than it looked between them. With a bright smile, she led the way to the second floor.

That should just about do it, Marc thought, glancing once more at his list. Or not, he added silently, his brow furrowing as one item among all the other, crossed-off ones drew his attention. Once again, he compared the list of stolen items with the list of those that were recovered.

"Is that all of it?" he asked Cary Owens, a fresh-faced rookie as he bounded down the stairs.

"Yessir," the officer said.

"Hmm."

"What?" Hallie asked, right on the heels of Owens and just in time to hear this last exchange.

Marc glanced up at her, standing on the staircase, her face shining with happiness.

"What is it?" she asked again.

"There's one thing that's not here." He didn't want to tell her, knew it would wipe that look of joy from her face. But he didn't have a choice. "Your scrapbook. It doesn't seem to be among the things we recovered."

He saw her hand tighten on the banister as alarm quickly replaced elation. "Oh, no."

"Damn," he muttered. "I could have sworn—" He turned again to Owens. "You're absolutely positive there was nothing else?"

"We got everything out of the perp's van, sir and into this one. Top to bottom. All of it. Didn't we?" He turned to his fellow officer, Ortega, who seemed to prefer that Owens do all the talking. When the other man nodded, Owens looked again at Marc and shrugged. "Sorry."

Marc couldn't miss seeing the way Hallie's shoulders slumped. From the heights of euphoria, she'd sunk to looking pained and lost. He wanted to do something for her, something that would give her hope. He went over to the staircase, offered his hand. "You okay?"

"What?" She looked down at his hand, took it and stepped down that last step as though in a daze. "I guess I assumed it was all here. That it—the scrapbook—would be in one of the boxes."

"No, ma'am," Owens said, his youthful face registering disappointment. "There was no scrapbook among the things we found."

"May I check?"

Quickly, she foraged through the boxes that lay scattered around the floor, but there was no scrapbook. Then she flew out of the museum. Marc followed and watched as she climbed into the van. Moments later, she climbed out again, dispirited, and slowly walked back toward him.

"Empty," she said.

"We'll find it," he assured her.

He saw hope flare briefly in her eyes. "Will you?"

"I'll do my best," he said, backtracking just a little, in the interests of honesty. "That I can promise you."

She kept her brave smile until a new thought struck. "I wonder why it's not here?"

He wanted to tell her not to worry, that no matter what, he'd get her precious scrapbook back to her. That she'd carried the burden of her family and her aloneness too long. That he was here now to take some of that burden away and take it on himself.

What was he thinking? Marc brought himself up short as he assessed where his mind was heading. He was here in an official capacity, returning stolen goods to a burglary victim, yet, inside, he was indulging in fantasy. A knight protecting his woman, like some Don Quixote of the hopeless. Which was insane, not only because he had no right to think of her as *his* woman—that matter had been settled already—but because both he and Hallie lived in the real world.

A world where a scumbag like Gus Madison, who would have found out from Tracy how much that scrapbook meant to her cousin, might have decided to avenge himself by hurting Hallie where it really mattered.

"Just don't give up," he told her, squeezing her hand once for comfort. "I'll question Madison, get the truth out of him."

"Will you?" Again, her brown eyes glowed with a small flicker of hope, followed by a look of such deep trust and confidence in him, he squirmed under their approval.

He coughed, then said, "I'll do my best."

"That's good enough for me."

She smiled mistily at him, and he felt his heart turn over with an emotion that was so sudden, and so strong, that he shook somewhere, deep inside.

His woman.

He'd had that thought just moments ago, and the phrase still resonated in his head, idiot that he was. How could Hallie be his woman, given her parameters? The man in her life must be willing to settle down, here in Promise. How could she be his woman when he'd already told her—and still meant it—that he wouldn't be staying?

But that didn't keep his imagination from taking wing, even allowing one corner of his mind to indulge in wishing things were different.

And wishes got you nowhere, he reminded himself, unconsciously quoting his father. So, ruthlessly ig-

noring this sudden appearance of an active fantasy
life, Marc nodded briskly to the two officers.

"Take the van back now, and get on with your
regular duties, okay? And thanks, men."

"You coming with us, sir?" Owens asked.

"No," he told them, surprising himself. "I'll walk
back in a little while."

"Yessir," Owens said, and he and Officer Ortega
took off.

After the two men left, Marc's insides remained
unsettled, and he found himself unable to stand still.
Leaving Hallie in the driveway, he strode into the
museum and prowled restlessly around the boxes on
the floor, picking each object up, studying it, then
setting it down again. Only the larger items, the oil,
the fireplace screen, a large tapestry, and the swords
had been taken upstairs; all the rest lay in disarray
around them.

"You're going to need some help getting this place
in order," he told her as she came through the door.

"Don't worry. Tracy and I will do it later."

"You said she's sick."

Shrugging, Hallie went behind the staircase and
opened a small door. "Then I'll do it myself."

He watched as she entered what seemed to be some
sort of broom closet. There she took some old rags
out of a bag and lifted a bucket filled with polish and
other cleaning gear.

As she exited the little room, he took the bucket
from her. "Why don't you and I do it together?" he
suggested.

"I can't ask you to do that."

"You didn't. I offered."

Wrinkles of worry creased her forehead. "Don't you have to get back to headquarters?"

"I'm the boss, remember? If they need me, they have my cell number," he said with a casual shrug. "Tell me what to do."

She gave him a shy smile. "Thanks."

For the next hour, they worked, side by side, carefully placing items back into their display cases, on the wall, in their niches. Marc climbed a ladder he found in the tool shed and hung both the tapestry and the large oil painting.

Hallie dusted and polished, and he heard her murmuring to her treasures as she did. They were an integral part of her, he realized more and more, extensions of her scrapbook. Roots. Something he'd never had and probably never would, given his lifestyle and plans for the future.

In a way, he envied her. His need for freedom, his lack of connectedness, which had always seemed a plus to him, began to seem tawdry somehow, an excuse that kept him from feeling part of the human race.

Except for the absence—temporary, she dearly hoped—of her family scrapbook, Hallie's heart felt lighter than it had in such a very long time. Her treasures had been returned, Tracy was safe, and Marc was working side by side with her, restoring her museum with her, looking after her in a way that she didn't remember ever being looked after.

Not for the first time, she experienced the temptation to just go up to him and lean on his massive chest and feel his strong arms around her, but, of course, she didn't give in to the urge. She thought of the portrait of great-great-great aunt Lizzie Palmer that hung downstairs on the main floor. Now there was a woman who never leaned on anyone or anything in her lifetime. *Oh, Lizzie,* Hallie thought with a loud sigh, *I wish I could be more like you.*

"More like who?"

She whirled around to bump smack into Marc, who had managed to come up behind her without her hearing him.

"Oops," she said and smiled up at him, but was arrested by the look in his eyes. What she saw was a hunger so unexpected and so fierce, she felt swept up in his pale, intense gaze. The next thing she knew, she'd wrapped her arms around his neck, stood on tiptoes, and offered her mouth.

Without hesitating, he took it. With a groan, his lips covered hers, his tongue seeking immediate entrance inside. She granted it with enthusiasm and reveled in the feel of its deep thrusts. She held on tight to the wide column of his neck as he pulled her closer to him. Blood rushed fiercely all throughout her body, and there was a tingling sensation in newly discovered nerve endings. Most of all, she felt the evidence of his desire for her pressing insistently against her stomach.

Oh, she thought, this is too wonderful. Her breathing accelerated in time with his and she ground her hips against him. It was almost as though, fully dressed, they were already joined. And, yes, she wanted to join with him. Oh, how she wanted…

"Hallie?"

Through a thick fog of desire, she heard a voice hailing her from somewhere far away, but she ignored it. Her hips continued to gyrate against Marc's taut body, and he groaned, louder now, with desire for her.

"Hallie?" Tracy called out again. "Are you upstairs?"

Hallie and Marc both froze in place.

"Yes?" she answered, reluctantly breaking their kiss.

"Where's the aspirin? I can't find it."

Reluctantly, Hallie stepped away from Marc. In the shadowed light of the wall sconces, his expression signaled frustration and regret, which was just how she was feeling. She stroked her fingers over his sculpted cheekbones.

"In my medicine cabinet," she shouted down to her cousin.

"I looked there."

Hallie smiled her apologies at Marc, then headed down the stairs. Tracy stood at the bottom, her nose red, her eyes streaming, a tissue clenched in her hand. She was wrapped in a faded, red plaid bathrobe and wore floppy pig slippers on her feet. She looked about twelve, Hallie thought.

"Hallie, I—" When Marc appeared, Tracy stopped. At first, she seemed taken aback. Then her gaze went from Hallie, back to Marc, and back to Hallie one more time. Dawning awareness appeared on her face.

"Uh-oh," she said. "I guess I interrupted you guys, huh? Sorry."

Hallie wasn't exactly embarrassed, but she did feel kind of awkward. "Marc," she began, then corrected herself. "Chief Walcott was just helping me put some of the things away."

"But I was going to do that with you."

Marc moved around Hallie, brushing briefly against her upper arm and setting her blood to racing again. As he came down the last step he said, "I decided to help in your place. You should be in bed," he went on briskly. "Not only for yourself, but so Hallie doesn't catch it."

At this paternal admonition, Tracy blew her nose, loudly, then stuffed the tissue in her robe pocket. "I was looking for the aspirin."

Hallie walked over to her cousin and put her arm through hers. "Come on, let's find that aspirin," she said cheerfully, heading for the museum door. Looking back over her shoulder, she raised an eyebrow in Marc's direction. "Coming?"

It was time for him to go, and Marc knew it. But he was still pretty shaken up from that kiss; besides, he didn't want to leave. Not yet. So, he followed the two women back to the house and sat at the kitchen table and watched while Hallie efficiently put the tea kettle on, then rifled through a small cabinet by the kitchen sink.

"I know I always keep some here. Yes, there they are. And vitamin C, too." Setting both bottles on the counter, she took two from each and handed them to Tracy. "Here. Take them right now."

Obediently, Tracy filled a glass with water and downed the pills while Hallie got out cups and a hand-painted tin container. "I'm making us some tea," she told Marc. "Care to join us?"

"Tea?"

She laughed at the horrified face he made. "Yes, tea. It's been around for years, you know, so there must be something to be said for it."

He chuckled at his own reaction. His mother used to make tea for him when he was sick, but he had never once chosen to drink it while healthy. Still, he liked sitting here in Hallie's warm, cozy kitchen, liked watching her fuss over her cousin. It seemed a tea kind of atmosphere, so he said, "Sure."

After the kettle whistled, Hallie poured hot water over the tea bags in each cup. Tracy took hers and smiled sleepily. "Well, listen, you guys, I'm going back to bed. So whatever, um, you two were doing. I mean, whatever you were up to. I mean—"

"We get the drift," Hallie said dryly. "Go on up. I'll bring you some chicken soup later."

Tracy walked away, sniffing all the while. In the doorway, she stopped, seemed to consider something for a moment, then turned around. Her dark blond hair hung lankly around her shoulders, her eyes and nose were red. But she gazed right at Marc and the determined look she gave him was no longer child-like. "Chief Walcott?"

"Yes?"

"Thanks for all you've done, for Hallie and for the museum. Thanks for taking it easy on me. I know I deserve to pay for what I did, and, believe me, I'm going to. Hallie and I have had some talks and I re-alize how badly I've acted," she went on earnestly.

"I'm sorry if I caused everyone trouble. I never meant to, but I know I did."

When she was finished, she took in a deep breath and waited to see if he had anything to say.

For the first time, Marc noticed the family resemblance. He was reminded, for a brief moment, of the way Hallie's face looked when she said something that was difficult for her.

Touched by the young woman's sincerity, he nodded. Maybe she would turn out all right after all. "Apology accepted."

"Thanks," she said gratefully.

"One more thing."

"Yes?"

"The scrapbook. It wasn't among the things we recovered."

"The scrapbook?" She looked at Hallie who stood, one hip propped against the counter, her teacup in her hand. "The family scrapbook? I didn't take that."

"What?" Hallie said.

"I mean, it wasn't on the list I gave Gus, anyway. Is it missing?"

"Yes."

"Oh, no. Oh, Hallie." Tracy's eyes were huge with guilt.

"Don't worry about it," her cousin said with a wave of her free hand. "Marc says we'll get it back."

"Oh, God, I think Gus might have taken more than he and I had talked about. I never did see all the stuff. He kept it all in his van." Her hand flew to her mouth in horror. "Oh, God," she said to Marc, "you're the police. I probably shouldn't be saying this to you. You'll want to reopen the case.''

"The case is closed. In the interests of getting your scrapbook back, all I want is anything that will help us find it.''

The young woman made a face of regret. "That's all I know. Sorry.''

"Go to bed,'' Hallie said. "Rest.''

Sniffling, Tracy shuffled out, her fuzzy pig slippers flopping around her feet. A fond expression on her face, Hallie watched her go, then sat down across from Marc.

"How's the tea?''

"Okay, I guess. Kind of tasteless.''

"Some people take lemon or sugar or milk or all three in theirs. Can I interest you in the first two? I'm out of milk.''

"Maybe a little sugar.''

Deep in thought, Hallie rose, got the sugar bowl, a spoon, and set them in front of him.

Since she and Marc had kissed, a mere ten minutes before, she had known what she had to do. It was in the forefront of her brain and had to be attended to. It wasn't going to be easy, but the voice inside her that had never led her wrong was pretty insistent.

She drank her tea for fortification. Marc surprised her by taking her hand, which rested on the tabletop, and squeezing it. "Are you going to be all right?'' he asked her.

"You mean about the scrapbook?''

"Yes.''

A reprieve, she thought, for a moment at least.

She considered his question before answering. "You know, in the scheme of things, it isn't a life and death situation. It's just memories, Marc, and—I'm amazed I'm actually saying this—but I don't feel nearly as desperate as I thought I would. I've looked at that thing so often that I have all the pictures in my head. Don't get me wrong. I hope we get it back. But if we don't, I'm not going to die of heartbreak."

"Good."

He took a sip of tea, but kept hold of her hand. She marveled at how small and pale her own looked in his much larger, darker one. Then she looked up at him, forced herself to meet his gaze and offered up a tentative smile.

"I love you, you know," she said.

At her words, Marc's eyes widened. He set his cup down with a clatter and he stared at her.

She waited, her pulse racing, for him to say something, anything, in response. But he just continued to stare at her, a frown forming between his eyebrows. She saw the muscles in his throat contract and expand as he swallowed.

"Wow," he said finally.

"It's okay," she said with more assurance and calm than she felt. "You don't have to say anything back, not if you don't want to."

He shook his head. "No, I want to. I'm just not sure what—" He thought about it a bit more, then said, "I'm not sure what love feels like. I mean, I know I have feelings for you, Hallie. Strong feelings."

"That's a start."

"But…it's all beside the point, isn't it?"

"Is it?"

"Isn't it?"

She gathered herself together before going on to the next part. "I've…found myself entertaining the thought of having an affair with you," she told him.

Again, he looked taken aback. "Have you?"

"Yes. I think—" she felt her cheeks redden, but went on anyway "—well, look what just happened upstairs. We're…both of us, crawling out of our skins. If we don't follow through, I'll always wonder what I missed. I haven't had a lot of experience, Marc. You can count the amount of lovers I've had on one hand. And I, well, sex has always been…pleasant, but I never quite knew what all the fuss was about. When you and I kiss, I think I have…an inkling." She smiled at her own understatement. "And I'd hate not to have that in my life."

In all his years, Marc had never been as thrown by a woman—hell, by anyone—as he was at this moment. Hallie was amazing, truly amazing. The guts it took for her to be saying this! "Wow," he said again.

The look on her face was at once wry, vulnerable, sweet, open, and brave. "I've never done anything like this before," she told him, "so I'm terrified."

"But you're doing great," he said, squeezing her hand.

"I've been thinking about what you said. About how we never know what's ahead, and why not grab all the happiness we can get, especially if it's put right in front of us? And well, I think you're right. I think maybe I've been a little too…rigid in my standards, in what I expect from a man. I've been too locked into having it all my way, you know, not being open. Maybe I'm supposed to have all kinds of lovers, all kinds of experiences, before settling down and having those kids." She shrugged. "I mean, who's to say?"

He felt his shoulders stiffen at the words "all kinds of lovers." No, he thought. She was not to have other lovers. Only him, dammit. No one else.

His woman.

He let go of her hand then rubbed his hand over his face. Expelling a breath, he said, "You astonish me."

"Is that good?"

His chuckle was rueful. "I have no idea. I also have no idea what to say now."

"Do you want me?"

She bit her lip after she said that. Her pretty face was aflame, and he suddenly understood what people meant when they said they wanted to laugh and cry at the same time. Had ever a sweeter proposition been made to a less deserving man?

"Oh, Hallie," he groaned, thoroughly undone. "Did you feel me when we kissed upstairs? Can you even begin to doubt when I want you so much it's killing me?"

She allowed herself a small, satisfied smile before she said, "Then, I guess the next move is up to you."

"To me?"

"I think I've said all I have to say, that I'd like to have an affair with you."

"You also said you loved me."

"I don't think I could want an affair if I didn't. Your turn."

"You're leaving it up to me?"

She nodded, then took her teacup and brought it over to the sink. He gazed at her back, and at the way her flyaway hair caught the slanting rays of the sun from a nearby window, creating glints of light all through the strawberry-blond strands. He noted the tense way she held her shoulders while he contemplated her offer.

Don't even think about it, soldier, he told himself. *A few more months, you're out of here, no looking back. And, no matter what the lady says about having lots of experiences, she'll fall apart when you do. She won't be able to handle it.*

And you won't either.

He felt a heaviness in his chest, a sense of deep loss. He'd never cried, not as a grown man. But he wished he could now, because maybe this heaviness would go away.

He had to do this. For her. For both of them. "Hallie?"

Slowly, she turned around, her face registering hope and dread at the same time.

With the utmost reluctance, he said, "Thank you, more than I can say, for your offer. I wish I could take you up on it, but I have to decline."

Chapter Ten

All Hallie could do was stare at Marc because she sure couldn't speak. It had been hard enough confessing her feelings for him, even more difficult letting him know she was ready for a physical relationship. But her reasoning had been that if men had to face rejection all the time, it was only fair that women put themselves through it, too.

And although she'd had some trepidation about taking this step, she hadn't really doubted the outcome. After all, she was quoting back at him the same reasoning he'd offered her—was it just last week?

But after putting her heart, her guts, her very soul on the line, he'd turned her down.

"You what?" she said finally.

He shook his head slowly. "I'm more sorry than I can say. Oh, God, Hallie, I want to. I mean, you don't know how much I want to. But it just wouldn't feel right. Nothing's changed. I'm still leaving. And if we get…involved, it'll rip us both apart.''

Then don't leave, she wanted to shout at him. *Stay here. With me!*

But she held her tongue. That would be begging, and she'd already lost any semblance of dignity she might have possessed.

She slumped against the kitchen counter. ''Just my luck,'' she said bitterly, ''to proposition someone who's decided to be noble.'' She put her hand over her eyes and shook her head.

He scrambled up from his chair and came over to her. ''Please don't cry.''

''I'm not crying. I'm just plain worn out. I haven't felt quite so…exposed in all my life.''

He put a hand on her shoulder. ''You were wonderful. Very brave.''

''Fat lot of good it did me. I'm beginning to think I'll never find a man who'll love me.''

His hand tightened. ''Don't,'' he said forcefully. ''Don't you dare think this has anything to do with whether or not you're loveable. You are. You're about the most loveable woman I've ever met.''

But you don't love me.

Turning her head away, she kept her mouth shut tight, so that little retort wouldn't come out, the way her unconscious thoughts sometimes did. She would *not* invoke pity. She wouldn't be able to handle his pity.

He brought his free hand up to her other shoulder and jerked her around to face him. ''It's me,'' he growled. ''I'm the one who's damaged. I was raised in a cold, disciplined household. I went from there to the military. I don't know how to let go enough to love. It's not you, it's me.''

''If you say so.'' She shook off his grip, which was painful enough to leave bruises. ''Look, why don't you just leave, okay? I think we've both said enough.''

''But—''

''Please, Marc. I'm tired.''

He stared at her for several moments, and she knew there was more he wanted to say.

But really, he'd said it all, hadn't he?

He nodded, then walked out the door.

''Hey, this isn't my order.''

Hallie gazed down at the plate her customer was pointing to. On it was an omelette, hash browns, a muffin. ''It's not?''

''I ordered oatmeal,'' the burly man said, clearly irritated, ''not eggs.''

''I'm so sorry, sir. I'll take care of that right away.''

As she passed another of her tables on the way back to the kitchen, another of her customers, a pregnant woman, called out, ''Miss, I've been waiting for my omelette for a long time.''

''Here it is,'' Hallie said, setting the plate down in front of her.

''Where's my french toast?'' her companion asked.

''Coming right up.'' She tried to sound cheerful, but a sob rose in her throat. Quickly, she hurried back to the kitchen, caught another of the waitresses by the arm and said, "Margie, please. Oatmeal on seven, french toast on ten. I'll be right back."

Before she disgraced herself in front of everyone, she ran out the back door, leaned against the tall garbage bin, put her face in her hands and wept.

Everything was wrong and she couldn't seem to make it right. Usually, no matter what was happening in her private life, she could be counted on to take care of her duties. But even that part of her life was falling apart.

She'd been unfocused and in a daze for several days now, since the conversation with Marc in her kitchen. It was like her head was somewhere else, in some other dimension. She'd lost her concentration, lost her ability to smile. At times she almost thought she was losing the will to live.

"Hallie?"

The timid voice behind her belonged to Tracy, who had begun to work as a hostess on the morning shift at Java, part of her cousin's newfound determination to earn her way and show Hallie that she could be responsible.

Keeping her back to her cousin, Hallie shook her head. "I'll be okay," she said through her tears. "Go back inside or Meg will wonder what's going on."

"She's the one who sent me out here. She's worried about you. So am I."

"I'll be fine. Go back inside."

Tracy didn't listen. Instead, she came around to face Hallie. "What's the matter? Please, tell me. Is it Marc?"

Hearing his name, Hallie's pain deepened and so did her sobs.

"Hallie?" Tracy said, then put her arms around her and held her. "It's okay. I'm here."

The final irony, Hallie thought. She, who was used to being the one to offer comfort to her cousin, was now being comforted by her. But it felt so good to be held, so she stayed where she was and let Tracy pat her on the back while she cried.

"There, there," Tracy murmured, as Hallie had said to her for so much of her life. "It's okay," she said again.

When at last the wave of sadness began to abate, she raised her head from Tracy's shoulder and offered her a teary grin. "Thanks, I needed that."

The younger woman's face showed concern. "Is it Marc?" she asked again. "I've heard you crying at night, and I was afraid to ask, but, well, you can talk to me. I mean, I understand about men and pain and all that."

Despite her tears, Hallie chuckled. "Yes, I guess you do. Neither of us has much luck in that department, have we?"

"Yeah, well, you've always been kind of picky, and I guess I haven't been picky enough. You love him, don't you?" When Hallie nodded, Tracy said, "Well, then, tell him."

"I already did."

"What did he say?"

"Not what I wanted to hear."

Her cousin's face fell. "Oh."

"Yeah. Doesn't look like there's going to be a happy ending."

"Oh, Hallie." Now Tracy's eyes filled. "That's so sad."

Hallie put her arm around her and squeezed. "Yeah, well, life is like that sometimes. And, I guess, we just have to keep plugging away. Come on, Tracy. Let's get back to work."

Marc drummed his fingers on his desk, then swiveled his chair around to look out at the ocean. The view from his office was one of the perks of his job— a sun-filled vista of a lone Monterey pine that sat on a bluff overlooking the ocean. Since he'd been in town, he'd often gazed out his window when troubled or feeling overwhelmed, and he'd find something out there that was soothing and eternal. Always it restored him, got him back on track.

But not today.

He was out of sorts, depressed.

He hadn't seen Hallie since the day she'd offered herself to him. Hadn't been back to Java, but had gone to another breakfast place, one that didn't have either the ambience or good food that he'd grown used to.

He was a coward, no doubt about it. But he couldn't bear to face her, couldn't tolerate the thought of seeing that sweet face of hers, couldn't stand being reminded of what he'd passed up.

He told himself it was the proper thing to do, but that didn't sit right. And he hadn't the foggiest notion of what to do about it.

He'd tried to make it up to her by finding her scrapbook, but that too hadn't gone well. Madison had disappeared. Marc had gone back to his San Francisco apartment three days in a row, but he hadn't shown.

As a parolee, he was supposed to notify his parole officer of any move, but he hadn't heard from him, either. Marc had requested that a warrant be issued, but he knew that finding one ex-con who wasn't even accused of anything much wouldn't be a major priority for the overworked police department, so he doubted much would come of it.

And it rankled. He couldn't let himself love Hallie and he couldn't find the one thing she prized most in the world. An honorable man, she'd called him. Ha. All in all, he felt like a big, fat failure.

A knock on his door woke him out of his reverie.

''Come in,'' he called out, swiveling back around in his chair and picking up a file on his desk, so he would look busy to whoever wanted to see him.

Len Baker, the city manager, walked in, a broad smile on his face.

''Len,'' Marc said, glad for the distraction. ''What brings you here? Grab a chair.''

Len sat across the desk from him, still smiling. ''I don't have much time. I just want you to know that I've been to visit Jack McKinney. He's in rehab, you know.''

''I'm glad he's feeling better.''

''Yes, well, he is. But he's also made a decision. He's definitely decided to retire.''

''I see.''

''Which means that we'll need to appoint a new

police chief. Now, I know you've told me this was temporary, but, well, the city council has instructed me to let you know that we think you're doing a whale of a job here, Captain.''

"Marc. How many times do I have to tell you that?''

"Probably a few more before it takes. Anyway, how about it? Interested in making it permanent?''

Marc was somewhat surprised by the offer. "What about Coe and Johnson? I'm sure they both still want the job.''

"Do they? Come on in, gentlemen,'' Len called out.

Bennett Coe and Frank Johnson came into the room. It was obvious they'd both been waiting on the other side of the door.

"Coe. Johnson,'' Marc said, nodding to the two police captains.

"Good afternoon, Chief,'' Coe said, while Johnson nodded.

They were both tall and fit, both in their early forties, one with steel-gray hair, the other with very little growth left on his head.

"I would tell you to take a seat,'' Marc said, "but they're both taken.''

"That's okay,'' Johnson said.

Len beamed at Marc. "Tell the chief what we've been talking about, men.''

Of the two captains, Coe had always been the one to give him the most trouble. His attitude had been, at times, belligerent and uncooperative, so it was with surprise that Marc heard him say, "Well, sir, we've been talking, Larry and me, and we want you to know that we've decided that you're the best man for the job."

"You've only been here a month or so," Johnson chimed in, "but we see how, with your experience, I mean your training in the Marines and all, well, people listen to you. You're tough but you're fair, too."

"One of us might want your job one day," Coe added, with a hint of his usual pugnacity, "but right now, well, we see how the wind is blowing, so, yeah, it's okay with us."

Johnson, always more of a mediator, shot his fellow captain a warning look, then turned to Marc. "If you do decide to take the job, we'll support you fully."

Marc propped his elbow on the arm of his chair and rubbed his mouth thoughtfully. This was totally unexpected, and he wasn't sure how to take it. He glanced at Len's smiling face, then at the visages of the two men who had obviously been told to shape up and accept the inevitable.

He nodded. "Thank you, men," he told the two captains, dismissing them. "I appreciate the vote of confidence," he added wryly.

Johnson and Coe exited, leaving Len and Marc alone in his office.

"Well?" Len said expectantly.

Marc stared at him, his mind reeling from the new developments. "I don't know, Len," he said finally.

The other man seemed disappointed. "Oh. I guess, I mean, it seemed that you were settling in so well. You seem to like it here."

"I do. It's a fine place."

"And, you seemed friendly with Hallie Fitzgerald." He winked. "I've heard a couple of rumors about the two of you."

Marc shifted in his chair. "Whatever you've heard is just that, rumors. Hallie and I are friends."

"Oh, I see," he said with a knowing grin. "Friends."

At that moment, Marc realized he did think of Hallie that way, as a friend. Despite what had happened between them. Maybe in time they could become friends again. She had qualities that mattered. She was loyal, someone to count on. He thought of some of their conversations together, where she'd lent an ear and hadn't judged him.

He'd always thought he couldn't be friends with a woman, but the direction of his thoughts was putting the lie to that theory.

Len rose from his chair. "Tell you what," he said heartily, like the good politician he was, "we have time. You take a few days, think about it."

"But—"

Len waved away his objection. "Never make important decisions on the spur of the moment. Well, gotta run."

And he was out the door.

Marc tried to focus on some paperwork, but soon there was a restlessness building inside that couldn't be ignored. After telling his secretary that he'd be gone for an hour or so, he went home, grabbed his leather bomber jacket and hopped on his Harley. Soon he was riding off into the hills east of town and up an old logging road he'd found on one of his previous outings.

He stopped at the top of the mountain and gazed around him. From this high vantage point, he peered out over the scene below. The brisk autumn day was clear, nary a cloud in sight. Spread out before him was the elegant Monterey Peninsula, the rugged cliffs of Big Sur, other small coastal towns like Promise. It was a view that rivaled any he'd seen in the rest of the world. Really, what more could any man want than this? he had to ask himself.

And where else in the world could he find a woman like Hallie, one who made him laugh, turned him on, and wasn't afraid of him? And one who, if he gave the two of them half a chance, would gladly give him children and make him a loving home?

But he had all these plans, all these dreams. He cherished his freedom.

You always had to pay a price for freedom. Was the price of freedom the forfeiture of love?

He didn't have answers, only questions. Troubled, he headed back to town. Before he returned to his office, he had one more stop to make.

"No, Gus, I mean it. I'm not going with you. Now leave."

Hallie looked at her cousin, who stood at the doorway with her arms crossed as she faced Gus Madison. The thin, bearded man had a mean, belligerent look on his face. Instead of going out the open front door, he came farther into the living room.

"Come on, Trace. You know you want to."

"I don't want to," Tracy said adamantly. "You lied to me, you got us in a whole bunch of trouble, and I don't even like you anymore."

"Now Trace," Gus said, walking toward her, his hands held out beseechingly. "I came all the way back here for you. I know you don't mean it. Come with me. I have lots of plans, but I want you along."

"What part of 'no' don't you understand?" Hallie said. From her position near the fireplace she'd been observing the exchange between Tracy and her ex-boyfriend and trying to stay out of it. But really, he didn't seem to be listening.

"You shut up, bitch," he said, turning to her, a look of pure venom on his face. "You started the whole thing when you refused to give Trace her money."

"Hey," Tracy said, "don't you dare talk to her like that."

"But, Trace," he said with a wheedling tone, and grabbed her.

She shook him off and ran over to Hallie. "You get out of here, Gus Madison, or we're going to call the police."

"You wouldn't dare," he sneered. Again, he rushed at her, yanking her by the arm.

"Hallie!" she called out as the ex-con was dragging her toward the open doorway.

Quickly, Hallie looked around the room for something to hit him with. Her gaze lighted on the antique hat rack that stood by the door. She dashed for it, lifted it up like a baseball bat, and said, "Let her go!"

But Gus wasn't listening. All his concentration was focused on pulling Tracy out the door. "Come on!"

"You asked for it!" Hallie swung with all her might and caught him on the shoulder.

He let go of Tracy and fell to the floor. In the next moment, he was scrambling to his feet and lunging for Hallie. She sidestepped him and brought the hat rack down on his head. Again, he fell to the floor, and this time he lay still.

"What the hell is going on here?"

Both Tracy and Hallie looked up to see Marc looming, big as life in the doorway.

"Marc!" Hallie cried, letting the hat rack crash to the ground as she ran over to him. He opened his arms and she went barreling into them.

"He was threatening me," Tracy said, looking at the still form of Gus Madison on the floor and then back at Marc. "Oh, God, Hallie, do you think you killed him?"

Just then, Madison groaned. Holding his head, he tried to sit up, but Marc gently moved Hallie to one side, walked over to him and put his foot on his chest.

"Just the man I want to see," he said calmly.

Madison, his eyes wild with fear, said, "Hey, that hurts."

"Does it?"

"Get off me."

"In a minute. First, tell me what you're doing here."

"He was going to kidnap me," Tracy offered.

"Was he?" Marc said, one eyebrow cocked.

"Bull," Madison said. "Get your foot off me. I can't breathe."

"Do you really want me to let you up?"

"Yes, dammit. I'm suffocating here."

"Are you? Tell you what. You tell me where the scrapbook is and I'll lift it off."

"What scrapbook?"

Marc cast a casual glance at Hallie who stared at them from the doorway. "Got any coffee, ladies? Looks like I'm going to be here for a while."

"I tell you, I don't know anything about some dumb scrapbook."

"Yes he does," Hallie said. "He described it to me over the phone."

With a growl, Marc took his foot off Madison's chest, then pulled the shorter man up by his shirt. He let him go, stood ramrod straight and gave him The Look. It was fierce and terrifying and even Hallie shrank back from its force.

Gus began to shake. "Okay, okay," he said, his hands held up defensively. "I tossed it."

"You what?" Marc's tone was menacing.

"I took it by mistake, I thought it was valuable. I tossed it over the side of the freeway."

Marc took a step toward him. "Where on the freeway?"

Again, Madison cowered. "Near the Harbor exit."

Marc nodded, then reached behind him and pulled out a pair of handcuffs. Within seconds, he'd turned Gus around and clapped them on him. "Tracy? Hallie? I take it you're willing to press charges this time? Assault and attempted kidnapping for starters."

"You betcha," Tracy said, then ran to her cousin and the two of them hugged each other.

Marc whipped out his phone, called HQ, and barked some orders into it.

After Madison had been taken away, Marc turned to Hallie and said "Come with me."

"Yessir," she said, still quivering inside, but willing to follow him to the ends of the earth. Her hero. He'd come to her rescue.

Outside, she hopped on the back of his Harley. He handed her a helmet and they took off.

She hugged him all the way through town, along the road that led to the freeway and then onto the 101. His leather jacket smelled old and positively wonderful. Despite the screen his back provided, the wind blew in her face as Marc took the curves at what seemed to be a dangerous angle, but she knew she was safe. He'd never let anything happen to her.

When they exited at Harbor, Marc stopped and gazed around them. As far as he could see, there were abandoned fields, dump sites filled with old cars and other refuse.

"Oh, dear," Hallie said, despair in her voice.

Determined, he started up the motorcycle again. "I'll go slowly. You look. What color was it?"

"Faded white with a yellow rose on the cover."

For a while, it seemed hopeless. They passed old vacuum cleaners, papers, toys. Then he felt Hallie stirring behind him.

"There!" she shouted. "Get closer to that bush, will you Marc?" When he pulled alongside a scraggly, mostly dead plant, she hopped off. "Marc! It's here!"

Quickly she bent down and picked up a large, fading, cloth-covered book, with a yellow rose stitched on its cover. He watched as she leafed through the pages.

"Some of the pictures are gone. They must have fallen out. But here's the wedding portrait of my grandparents. And one of my mother at her christening. Oh, Marc." With tears of happiness in her eyes, she gazed at him. "Thank you."

He felt his chest fill with satisfaction. "Tomorrow, we'll come back with some volunteers and comb the area. We'll get most of it back, I promise."

"Oh, Marc," she said again. Clutching the scrapbook to her chest, she walked over to him and buried her face in his chest.

He closed his eyes and said a silent prayer of thanks to a God he didn't know if he believed in or not.

Hallie was overwhelmed with feelings, so for a little while, it didn't register that Marc seemed to be shaking. She raised her head and stared at him. "What is it?"

It was a moment before he answered her. "I was so scared."

"You, scared?"

"As I was coming up the walkway, I heard Gus threatening the two of you. I was afraid I wouldn't get there in time. I thought my heart would stop."

"Oh, Marc."

"Hallie."

He dismounted the bike, took the scrapbook and set it on the seat, then put his arms around her and held her again. They stood there, together, in a field of abandoned possessions.

Not for the first time, she drew strength from this man. She owed him so much. He'd given her an amazing gift—he'd returned her memories to her.

"You know something?" he murmured into her hair after a while.

"What?"

"I love you."

She lifted her head and stared at him, her mouth ajar.

"I was so scared of losing you, it almost killed me." He smiled, and there was a glint of tears in his hazel eyes. "I figure that's got to be love."

Joy burst in her, so strong she thought she might be able to fly. "Sure sounds like it."

"I'd like to take you up on your offer." He took a strand of her hair and wound it around his finger.

"Which one was that?"

"To have an affair, with honorable intentions."

"An affair with honorable intentions," she repeated.

"I would ask you to marry me right now," he said earnestly, "but I think it's a little soon."

"M-m-marriage?" Again, her jaw dropped. Would wonders ever cease? "I don't remember mentioning marriage."

"Well, I'm mentioning it."

"But, what about your plans?"

"They've changed." He gripped her upper arms

and went on. "I tell you, Hallie, when I realized how much you mean to me, it's like a whole new world opened up. See, I think I've had it all backward. I thought I wanted to travel. But all I did in the military was travel. I'm afraid of setting down roots, but all I've done my whole life was not set down roots. I thought I was missing a sense of freedom, but all I've had is freedom, and I was miserable, although I didn't know it."

"Oh, Marc." She stroked his cheek. At this moment, this big, tough, burly man looked so vulnerable, so exposed, she thought her heart would break.

"What I've missed isn't freedom," he went on, "but giving myself permission to land in one place and stay there. I've had this…emptiness inside me my whole life. As far back as I can remember I felt like an outsider. But that's because I've kept myself outside. And I've kept myself outside because I always knew I was leaving."

"Yes," she said softly.

He let go of her arms, stared off into space. "So I've been thinking. What if I try it differently this time, try it the regular, normal way? Marriage, a home, kids." He frowned. "Although I'm still not sure what kind of father I'll be."

"You'll be a wonderful father."

"Yeah, well, I have this temper."

"And you know how to control it. Don't you see? I'm not afraid of you, our children won't be either, promise."

His frown deepened and he looked at her accusingly. "Why aren't you afraid of me? Did you see the way Gus almost peed in his pants? Why don't I have that effect on you?"

She laughed. "Do you want to?"

"Yes. No." He paused, then said sheepishly, "No."

"Then, that's why. I know you don't mean it. With me, I mean. You're a softy, Marc Walcott."

"Damn," he muttered, and he was only half kidding. "You see right through me."

"And aren't you glad I do." She pulled his head down and kissed him. It felt so lovely, so right, so real.

He moved his mouth over her face, her nose, her forehead. "I'll be staying in Promise. They want me to take on the police chief job permanently."

"Well, good," she murmured back, feeling that if the world ended right that moment, it would be fine.

He kissed her again, took her face between his hands and grinned. "So, are you my girl?"

She grinned back at him, relaxed and full and complete. "That I am," she said. "That I am."

* * * * *

Your opinion is important to us! Please take a few moments to share your thoughts with us about your experiences with Harlequin and Silhouette books. Your comments will be very useful in ensuring that we deliver books you love to read. *Please take a few minutes to complete the questionnaire, then send it to us at the address below.*

Send your completed questionnaires to:
Harlequin/Silhouette Reader Survey, P.O. Box 9046, Buffalo, NY 14269-9046

1. As you may know, there are many different lines under the Harlequin and Silhouette brands. Each of the lines is listed below. Please check the box that most represents your reading habit for each line.

Line	Currently read this line	Do not read this line	Not sure if I read this line
Harlequin American Romance	❑	❑	❑
Harlequin Duets	❑	❑	❑
Harlequin Romance	❑	❑	❑
Harlequin Historicals	❑	❑	❑
Harlequin Superromance	❑	❑	❑
Harlequin Intrigue	❑	❑	❑
Harlequin Presents	❑	❑	❑
Harlequin Temptation	❑	❑	❑
Harlequin Blaze	❑	❑	❑
Silhouette Special Edition	❑	❑	❑
Silhouette Romance	❑	❑	❑
Silhouette Intimate Moments	❑	❑	❑
Silhouette Desire	❑	❑	❑

2. Which of the following best describes why you bought *this book?* One answer only, please.

the picture on the cover	❑	the title	❑
the author	❑	the line is one I read often	❑
part of a miniseries	❑	saw an ad in another book	❑
saw an ad in a magazine/newsletter	❑	a friend told me about it	❑
I borrowed/was given this book	❑	other: _____	❑

3. Where did you buy *this book?* One answer only, please.

at Barnes & Noble	❑	at a grocery store	❑
at Waldenbooks	❑	at a drugstore	❑
at Borders	❑	on eHarlequin.com Web site	❑
at another bookstore	❑	from another Web site	❑
at Wal-Mart	❑	Harlequin/Silhouette Reader	❑
at Target	❑	Service/through the mail	
at Kmart	❑	used books from anywhere	
at another department store or mass merchandiser	❑	I borrowed/was given this book	❑

4. On average, how many Harlequin and Silhouette books do you buy at one time?

I buy _____ books at one time	❑
I rarely buy a book	❑

MRQ403SR-1A

5. How many times per month do you shop for any *Harlequin and/or Silhouette* books?
   One answer only, please.

1 or more times a week	❑	a few times per year	❑
1 to 3 times per month	❑	less often than once a year	❑
1 to 2 times every 3 months	❑	never	❑

6. When you think of your ideal heroine, which *one* statement describes her the best?
   One answer only, please.

She's a woman who is strong-willed	❑	She's a desirable woman	❑
She's a woman who is needed by others	❑	She's a powerful woman	❑
She's a woman who is taken care of	❑	She's a passionate woman	❑
She's an adventurous woman	❑	She's a sensitive woman	❑

7. The following statements describe types or genres of books that you may be
   interested in reading. Pick *up to 2 types* of books that you are most interested in.

   I like to read about truly romantic relationships ❑
   I like to read stories that are sexy romances ❑
   I like to read romantic comedies ❑
   I like to read a romantic mystery/suspense ❑
   I like to read about romantic adventures ❑
   I like to read romance stories that involve family ❑
   I like to read about a romance in times or places that I have never seen ❑
   Other: _____ – ❑

*The following questions help us to group your answers with those readers who are
similar to you. Your answers will remain confidential.*

8. Please record your year of birth below.
   19 ____

9. What is your marital status?
   single ❑   married ❑   common-law ❑   widowed ❑
   divorced/separated ❑

10. Do you have children 18 years of age or younger currently living at home?
    yes ❑   no ❑

11. Which of the following best describes your employment status?
    employed full-time or part-time ❑   homemaker ❑   student ❑
    retired ❑   unemployed ❑

12. Do you have access to the Internet from either home or work?
    yes ❑   no ❑

13. Have you ever visited eHarlequin.com?
    yes ❑   no ❑

14. What state do you live in?
    _____

15. Are you a member of Harlequin/Silhouette Reader Service?
    yes ❑   Account # _____   no ❑   MRQ403SR-1B